Pride

GRACE FAY

ISBN:
ISBN-13:

DEDICATION

For Saqqara and Cleopatra, in the hope they have good cubs.

CONTENTS

	Acknowledgments	viii
1	The Dream	1
2	First glimpse Realised	6
3	Come With Me	10
4	Finding Saqqara	15
5	An Explanation	18
6	Shot	27
7	Suspension	31
8	She Walks Beside You	36
9	Rage and Power	45
10	The Influence of Mejia	50
11	Becoming	53
12	Idurna Idarya	56

13	We Must Walk	69
14	The Boy	72
15	Ida	75
16	Walking with Saqqara	83
17	Hostile Thoughts	88
18	The Longing Feeling	97
19	Darla	104
20	Discovery	109
21	Leaving	114
22	Capture	116

PRIDE

ACKNOWLEDGMENTS

With heartfelt thanks to Patience, for investing her time in me and giving me constructive criticism. My teacher Mrs Murphy for instructing me in many of the writing techniques that I have used in this book. You have always been encouraging and supportive of my writing.

Chapter One

The Dream

It was his land, his home, his kingdom. No-one could take it from him. On the crest of the hill he stood; tall; strong; majestic; behind him, the blazing, crimson sun rose up out of the black, rippling sea, spreading its warming light over the dark earth.

He turned his face towards the west, yet he was not silhouetted against the rising sun.

The light shone through his mane, through his fur, giving the illusion that he was enveloped in a corona of shining white light -

the same colour of his fur - yet though he had all these wondrous qualities, there was something missing. His golden eyes, beautiful and sad, shone with glittering tears.
He was lonely.

Stalking down from the hill, into a concealing thicket of African bush, he began to lick himself, his rough tongue taking care of any dirt nestling deep in his pale fur.

Staring at the colour-filled sunrise, amber eyes reflecting the deep reds, bright yet muted oranges and calm, complimenting yellows; he felt a light, warm breeze ripple his mane. Leisurely he lay there; breath misting in the relatively cool morning; fur undulating slightly; golden-amber eyes facing west again. He seemed closer than before. As he opened his mouth, a glint of white teeth registered inside. A roar issued from his jaws. In that one tumultuous cry, though, there were words.

"I am Saqqara!"

Gasping and sweating, Tau Oyenusi sat bolt upright in her bed. *Him*, she thought, *again.* She tossed back the brightly coloured woven blankets and stepped out of bed.

"MEOW!"

"I'm so sorry, Lioness!"

Lioness, Tau's cat, hissed and stalked off, her recently stepped on pale ginger tail waving high in the air. Walking across the rough, highly textured rag rug, the colourful strips of fabric tickling her toes, Tau stared out of the large window at the yellows, greens and browns of the bush, the sun almost fully risen on the horizon.

Suddenly, something weighed down Tau's arms. Instinctively, she cradled it, realising it was Lioness. Wrapping her furry tail around Tau's forearm, Lioness gazed up at her with amber eyes.

"The lion…" breathed Tau.

Lioness, oblivious to her mistress' voice, began to purr. Looking out of the window again, Tau noticed a pair of slanted golden eyes staring at her from a patch of browning grass. Startled, she dropped Lioness, who hissed indignantly and ran off, but Tau barely noticed. Quickly, she scanned the bush, but there was no sign of the haunting golden eyes.

"Lioness, don't jump on me…… get off…" The sleep–slurred voice belonged to Darlene, Tau's mum. There was a thump and yet another hiss. Turning around, Tau caught sight of Lioness scooting under her mum's bed, her almond-shaped eyes glowing in the dark space.

"Sorry about Lioness, Mum, she's in one of her moods. It's a cat thing." Tau apologised.

Darlene laughed.

"Tau, don't worry, you know I don't care unless Lioness does something naughty, and I needed to get up anyway."

Climbing out of bed and smoothing down the thin patchwork quilt, Darlene's slippered feet padded across the rug to put an arm around her daughter's shoulders.

"I had the dream about the lion again, Mum. Sometimes they're in different places, different things happen, but its always, always the same lion." Tau said.

"What did it look like, Tau?" queried Darlene.

"No, not *it*, *he*. *He* was white, Mum," answered Tau, "and he had golden eyes."

Tau's honey-coloured gaze wandered back to the brown patch of grass in which she had first seen the lion's haunting yellow pair. Taking advantage of her sudden lapse into silence, Lioness crept out from under the bed and pawed her way across the carpet, before entwining herself around Tau's ankles, rubbing against her calves. Reaching down to pick her up, Tau gently scratched her behind the ears.

"Guess you aren't cross with me any more, eh?" Tau ruffled the fur on her back. Loud, satisfied purring answered her.

"I guess that's a yes then!" laughed Tau. Lioness leapt lightly onto the rug, padding over to Tau's bed to curl up on the pillow, leaving Tau to absent-mindedly stare out of the window once again, carefully examining the beautiful landscape of the Timbavati region of Africa.

Chapter Two

First Glimpse Realised

"He's real...." Tau breathed, glancing out of the glass again. A tufted tail flicked out of sight behind a bush. Moments later, the grass rippled as something large stalked away from the window. The white, tufted tail waved in the air above the dry, yellowish grass, as if tempting Tau to run after it. A pair of amber eyes glaring out of a patch of thorns were the only sign that anything had been there; then they weren't there anymore.

"Gone…" murmured Tau. Padding slowly away from the window, pulling the thin sackcloth curtains shut as she went, Tau flumped down onto her bed. A small cloud of dust rose from the depression she had made in the crocheted woollen blankets. They needed a clean. Getting up, Tau made her way downstairs, wisps of dust swirling up from the ancient stair carpeting (once white, now a slightly sickly yellowish-cream colour) at each step. Slipper-soles whispering on the unglazed ceramic tiles of the slightly rustic, cobbled-together kitchen floor, the weaved , dry-as-a-bone palm leaf matting in the centre not making much difference to the noise either, Tau's feet rustled as she made her way to her mum, who happened to be peeling a mango with a small knife by the sink. Tapping her on the shoulder, Tau asked

"What's for breakfast, Mum?"

Startled, Darlene jumped, causing the knife to clatter into the sink - scratching the ceramic a little - and the mango to slide across the worktop, fall off the end and land with a quiet splat on the tiled floor.

As Darlene bent to retrieve it, she reproved,

"Goodness, girl, you just made me drop it!"

Suddenly, Lioness bounded in through her cat-flap in the back door, raked

Tau's slippers and immediately pounced upon the dropped mango.

"Lioness! Lioness, get off that! It's our breakfast!" Darlene dragged Lioness off the floor and passed her to Tau. While she struggled to hold her, Darlene scooped the slightly mangled, half-peeled mango off the tiles and retrieved the little knife from the sink, before continuing to peel it as if nothing had happened.

With Lioness still squirming to get loose, Tau hefted the cat back upstairs, and by the time she was at the top Tau was coughing violently from all the dust they'd dislodged. As she opened the door to her shared attic bedroom, she sighed. That horrid dust was one thing you couldn't get away from in Africa. The sandy, gritty substance got everywhere: embedded in your hair, stuck under your nails, coating every surface with a layer of yellow. That's what had happened to the stairs.

Thankfully, their bedroom was less dusty because the curtains filtered the air slightly. Unfortunately, now normal dust accumulated everywhere as Darlene 'forgot' to dust it because she didn't like cleaning. Tau flopped down onto her bed and lay down on top of the covers. Lioness, lust for mango flesh momentarily forgotten, climbed up onto the bed and curled up on the pillowcase , her long, ginger tail tickling Tau's dark cheek. Tau whispered to her "I wish I could see my lion again. I wish you could talk, so you could tell me where he is. But you are just a cat, and you can't…"

"Ah, but I can Tau, I can…" purred Lioness.

Chapter Three

Come With Me

"But….. how?" enquired Tau , utterly incredulous.

"No time for the whole story, I don't even know myself," answered Lioness, simultaneously licking her claws, "I just can."

"Well," conceded Tau, "If you can talk, you must know more than most humans, right?"

"I hate to boast, " purred Lioness thoughtfully ,"But, yes ,Tau, I believe you are correct."

"So can I ask you a few questions, please?"

"Of course."

"First, am I dreaming?"

"No, but if you want to check, stroke me." suggested Lioness.

Tau obliged, ruffling her silky ginger and cream fur, surprised to find her cat was completely solid.

"Okay, I'm not dreaming. Second, where do you go at night?"

She looked affronted. "How do you know I go anywhere at night?"

"Sometimes I wake up early, and you aren't there, then I go back to sleep and wake up in the morning and there you are, by my bed, all ready to be stepped on."

"And all the bruises that gave me," sighed Lioness, "You really must learn to be more careful, Tau."

"Where do you go at night?" prompted Tau.

"Oh, alright.... " moaned an exasperated Lioness, "I was seeing the lion - Saqqara."

"Wha - o my - wait a sec -" Tau was flabbergasted, speechless. Finally, she found her voice.

"You've got a crush on my lion?"

Lioness raised her eyes to the ceiling.

"I knew you would take it like this. For your information, I do not have a crush on Saqqara. We were just talking. We're very closely related, you know. As a species. Only three letters between us." Her furry face went a slightly darker ginger.

"You're blushing……"sniggered Tau.

Now irritated, Lioness retorted, "Do you want to know where he is or not? Or shall I just walk away and never come back?"

"Show me where he is!"

"Say please."

Annoyed at being treated like a small child, Tau grudgingly obliged.

"Show me where he is……please."

"Place your hand on my back, shut your eyes and feel my heart."

Though a little confused, Tau did as she asked. Immediately, image after unfamiliar image flashed before her eyes. She was padding through the grass, a thrill racing in her veins. She froze, her nose twitching in the dim light of morning. Then she saw *him*. She felt her eyes widen, and the thrill sprinting through her intensified. Metres away, half-hidden in the gently waving greenish-yellow grass was a beautiful lion.

And not just any old lion. Silky-soft , pure white fur coated every inch of his sleek body, and his great, white mane wafted slightly in the light breeze. At that moment, he roared tumultuously, causing her to start and run away.

Then Tau was back in her little attic room, breathing heavily, and staring at Lioness.

"What.........was...........that thing........ you just........did?" asked Tau, breathing between each word. (she had a stitch, as though she had run for miles.)

"I showed you the morning on which I first saw Saqqara." She licked her paws, then proceeded to rub her ears. Suddenly she paused, licked her nose, and purred,

"Put your hand on my back again, and I'll show you where he is."
Tau eagerly obliged.

"And don't forget to close your eyes."

Tau had already done so. Tau was running through the bush, seeing everything through feline, almond-shaped eyes; dodging thorns; leaping over tall patches of grass; nose sniffing eagerly; ears twitching wildly, trying to catch a noise she couldn't hear in their silky nets.

Suddenly, she caught sight of something staring at her from out of a bush. It was a pair of amber eyes! Sneaking round to the right side of the eyes, she saw it was Saqqara.

Tau was back in her room, breathing heavily for the second time in as many minutes.

"Where is he? How far did we go?" Tau clamoured.

Lioness looked at her serenely through her almond-shaped eyes.

"Saqqara," she said, her eyes lighting up, "Is five yards away, near a small waterhole, and is facing north-north-west."

Chapter Four

Finding Saqqara

"Then we need to get to him! Come on Lioness, let's get going!" exclaimed Tau, eager to start.

"Wait a second, Tau, we need to devise a plan to get out of here without disturbing your mum," chided Lioness. Tau was rushing around the small bedroom, picking up various items and stuffing them into an old, purple backpack, but when she reached for Lioness (to put her gently in the bag, as she usually did when she travelled) she raked her with her claws and reminded Tau.

"I'm not your dumb old cat anymore, Tau!"

"Alright, alright, I'm not used to this

yet!"

"Now get that backpack on your back *now*, and I'll go and scout. I won't be noticed as much. Three meows will be your signal to go." With that, and a wave of her tail, she was gone.

Twenty minutes later, three piercing meows echoed through the house.

Without pausing for a moment, Tau sneaked downstairs and out of the back door, where Lioness was waiting, flicking her tail impatiently.

"You were *ages*……"she reproved.

Tau defended herself by saying, "I had to get past Mum, and she's got eagle eyes!"

Undeterred, Lioness went on, "Fibber! Darlene was, and is, on the sofa, snoring, so what were you doing?"

"I was……"Tau's voice trailed off as her eyes raised to the space behind Lioness.

Annoyed at this lack of excuse, Lioness repeated, "What were you doing?"

"Shhhh! Stay very still…"hissed Tau.

"What?" whispered Lioness.

"Saqqara is right behind you."

Slowly, they turned around, and

stared at the huge white lion barring their path. She looked into his beautiful golden eyes.

"Hello," said Tau Oyenusi.

The lion blinked, and for a terrible moment, Tau thought it might not be him. Then he nodded, as if acknowledging her presence, and replied in a deep, rumbling voice, "Tau. I have dreamed of you."

Chapter Five

An Explanation

"Lioness. You are her friend, I take it?" asked Saqqara.

"Until recently her cat, but now her friend."

"Ummmmm.........Lioness?" whispered Tau out of the corner of her mouth, "Is this really happening, and, if so, how and why?"

Lioness laughed, sounding surprisingly human, considering she was a cat. "Tau, this is really happening, but it's a long story, so I will explain."

"Explain then." said Tau curtly.

"You have a mind bond with Saqqara. This means you can share memories and scape-sight – which is what I used to find Saqqara - although you cannot communicate telepathically, that is to say, through thought. In some interesting cases, however, some pairs have been able to dream of one another, which, I gather, is what you first did to find Saqqara."

"But how did you-"

Tau was cut short, though, as Lioness had anticipated her question.

"Anyone can do it, you just need to concentrate extremely hard. And I'll tell you a secret, Tau. When I was using scape-sight in your bedroom, when you could feel my heart and see my memories, I wasn't actually there at all. I was running through the bush, just as you were, through my mind and my eyes, keeping the mental link between my mind and yours."

Tau turned to Saqqara.

"Saqqara. I have dreamed of you."

She smiled, and the light breeze rippled her long, black hair. A moment of peaceful silence, then he roared to the sky, and she likewise. Abruptly, the roar stopped.

Something was different about the landscape. Saqqara motioned to Tau. “Come here, child. Place your hand in my mane and shut your eyes.” Tau needed no prompting, burying her hands deep in his soft, silky white mane.

“Lioness, curl up on my back.” Lioness bounded up onto Saqqara’s shoulders.

Suddenly, they were sneaking through the dry, whispering grass. Footsteps reverberated through the landscape and shouts could be heard. The dull silver shine of a gun barrel winked for a moment in the bright sunlight. That was all he needed.

“Hunters or – maybe and - trappers. They want pelts. Fur pelts.” Saqqara was a strong young lion, in his prime, but now he was trembling. And it certainly wasn’t cold. Over the horizon, dark black silhouettes could already be seen.

“Lioness, can I have a word?” Saqqara and Lioness walked about a hundred metres away before starting to talk. Tau sat down on the hard, compacted ground. Dust swirled around her ankles. Strange. There was no sign of a breeze. Tau licked her index finger and held it up. No, there was most definitely no sign of wind, not even the slightest, lightest draft.

Without warning, the sand rose up and solidified into the form of a woman. She had long, sandy-blonde hair with streaks of white-blonde and darker blonde running through it, tanned but obviously pale skin and the most startling sapphire-blue eyes. Tau's mother had an old sapphire ring at home, but this woman's eyes had a sparkling star in their depths, and were by far brighter than the pale, stark hardness of that ancient bronze ring.

The woman seemed to be dressed in a yellow fabric that was constantly moving and shifting in the wind. She smiled at the look of curiosity on Tau's face, and the sunlight bounced off her white teeth. Stepping closer, Tau saw the fabric was made of sand, desert sand.

"Who are you?" Tau asked.

"I am Aleesa, the One Being of Africa." The woman's voice was like the music that Tau played on the little wooden whistle she had been given for her eleventh birthday. But she was still confused.

"What's a One Being?"

"It means that I was here before." Aleesa answered.

"Before what?"

"Everything. I was born of the Sea of Night, and Amala, the Lady of the Moon, just as all One Beings are. And though we are related, we are divided. Mejia, the One Being of the Arctic, is as cold and ruthless as the ice with which her palace is made. I came to tell you something other than that, though. When you speak to Lioness, to Saqqara, you are speaking Lion. Your *inama,* your soul-creature, is a lioness. Her name is Nevadra. If you lose her, you will be gone."

"What would happen if you did lose your *inama*?" queried Tau.

"You would become a Suspended. You would not be dead, but you would not be truly alive, either. It would be like a coma, but if someone put their hand or ear to your chest, they would not hear a heartbeat, but the keening whine of your *inama* calling to your heart. You would pass into Suspension, the land between the worlds. People who have been there and returned, that is to say, have artificial souls, or are lucky enough to have their *inamas* returned to them, say it is like a hospital ward, large and white and sterilised.

But they were wrong. Those must have been very distant dreams."

"What's Suspension like?" asked Tau, eager for more information.

"I have been there, so I know."

"What! But I-"

Aleesa laughed, and the sounds of the first rains of spring filled the air.

"I am a One Being, and I was here before everything and anywhere, so I may go anywhere and see and feel everything."

Suddenly there came the crunch of booted feet snapping blades of dry grass.

Aleesa's body dissolved into a million tiny grains of sand and blew away in the sudden wind, leaving behind the words, "I must not be seen! Hunters are coming! Hide in the tall grass behind you!"

Tau hadn't noticed, but, as Aleesa had said, tall grass grew behind her. She dove into it, and suddenly Saqqara was there, roaring with all his strength and scratching and biting the hunters. They (the lion and the hunters) looked so entangled and hurt that Tau couldn't help but shout "Stop, stop! You'll hurt them and then they'll hurt you and – oh, just stop!" She tried to pull Saqqara back, but it was no use, then, he did. Breathing heavily and with his golden eyes blazing, Saqqara backed down into a crouch position. For a moment, Tau thought that the hunters weren't going to catch Saqqara, but then they threw a heavy rope-and-steel net over them both. Thinking quickly, Tau remembered the pocket knife that Darlene had given her. She wriggled her hand into the pocket of her jeans and triumphantly yanked the little silver-and-red blade out. Craning her neck round, she saw that Saqqara was thrashing, ripping, biting at the net, trying to get free, but the more he tried to rip through the trap, the more hopelessly entangled he became.

Knowing that he would exhaust himself with his efforts, Tau, thinking that this would calm him, put a hand in his mane and stroked the long, white fur. Saqqara relaxed, breathing deeply, onto the crushed desert grass beneath him. Lioness leapt lithely through a hole and curled up next to Saqqara's right foreleg. As though he could not bear it any longer, though, Saqqara pounced forward as far as he could and redoubled his attempts to bite and scratch the trappers. Instantly, panic was unleashed. The sounds of grass being flattened mingled with roaring as a blur of fur and claws and steel-toe-capped boots erupted in the space around Tau and Lioness. Somehow, Tau managed to use her little pocket knife to saw a hole in the thick weaved-rope-and-steel net and struggle out of the small, ragged hole she had made.(The knife was now, unfortunately, quite bent and twisted due to its rough treatment.) Leaping out of the gap after her, Lioness rushed to Saqqara's side, adding her own flashing claws and snapping teeth to the fray. As she attacked ankles and leapt at faces, a stray gun barrel smote her on the side of her head and she was knocked to the ground. She shook herself vigorously and leapt up again, seeming to become fiercer, to want revenge for this initial wound. Tau sought to add her own strength to the battle, hitting, missing and kicking wherever she could.

One of the trappers, young, with brown hair and sharp, eagle-like greyish-yellow eyes, was kicked in the stomach, hard, and fell backwards, winded, onto the dry plains ground. Clutching his gun as it rocked in his hands, he gripped it tightly, and, utterly by accident, squeezed the trigger. He had forgotten he had a bullet in the firing chamber. The barrel of the gun was pointing straight at Tau. The bullet rushed towards her through the air, for a moment Tau thought she saw Aleesa. She shot a bolt of sand at it, trying to stop it, but instead the bullet turned it black and absorbed the gritty substance into itself and carried on in its journey of death.

Chapter Six

Shot

As the bullet thudded into Tau's chest, for a moment she did not feel anything at all, but that was only for a second. The next, pain exploded in Tau's chest, a crimson stain spreading across the front of her top. Then the world seemed to dissolve and crack into millions of misty shards and then darkness surrounded her and swallowed her up.

Everyone froze. "Jonathan, what have you done?" gasped one of the hunters. A short conversation of Lion passed between Lioness and Saqqara. Lioness received a nod from Saqqara. She looked straight into the hunters' eyes and said, "You have inflicted serious harm on my friend. She may die. You must carry her back to her mother's house, which is close by. Do not tell anyone that I can speak. Do as I say."

The young hunter spoke up. He was clearly in shock at what he had done.

"B-But what a-about the l-lion?" he stammered.

"Saqqara?"

Another man, with curly red hair and a beard, looked utterly incredulous.

"That *thing*, that huge, monstrous *beast*, has a *name*?"

"Yes I do," growled Saqqara, "and I would thank you to use it." And he took the man's head in his jaws and held it there for about two seconds without biting him, before releasing him by opening his mouth and dropping the trembling hunter onto the ground, where he collapsed in a crumpled, shaking heap.

"There. That's what might happen to you. Now *do as she says.*"

Although he spoke softly, there was unspeakable menace enclosed within

Saqqara's words. The hunters moved to pick up Tau, but Saqqara gently cuffed them down.

"Let me. You may drop her. Place her on my back. Gently, mind."

So Tau was placed on Saqqara's back with her head between Saqqara's shoulder blades. Padding slowly so as not to jog Tau, he found his way back to the window where he had first seen her. Lioness jumped up to open the door and the procession trooped in, setting Tau down on the palm matting in the kitchen, leaving a note which read: *Care for her. She has been shot in the chest.*

Lioness curled up beside her and told Saqqara and the hunters to wait outside. Footsteps came down the stairs and Darlene entered the kitchen and screamed. Then she sank down and wept into the sink. Looking more closely at her daughter, she saw the note.

Quickly, she gently scooped up Tau into her shaking arms and carefully carried her limp child up the stairs, placing her on top of her bed but without pulling the sheets over her. Darlene drew the curtains to shut out a little of the choking dust. She checked they were properly shut, then turned her attentions to Tau. Undoing the buttons of her top, Darlene inspected the wound. It was quite deep and black cobwebs stretched out from it and across Tau's chest and they were slowly spreading. And all the time her eyes were misting over and the mist was getting thicker by the minute, but she was still breathing, thank goodness. Darlene found some pristine(ish) white bandages and wrapped Tau's chest in them. Days passed, but Tau did not die, but her condition did not improve either; neither did she awaken. But then something happened, and even if Darlene had known, she saw there was something wrong.

Chapter Seven

Suspension

Tau had passed into Suspension. The bullet had been poisoned when Aleesa had tried to stop it hitting Tau. Somehow, the poison had forced Nevadra, Tau's *inama*, out of her body. She was now only a phantom of her former self.

Suspension was like a sea of thoughts, sharing, mingling and being heard, and would have been pleasant, if not for the oil slick spreading across the surface and spiralling down into the dark and treacherous depths. It was this that was poisoning the land. What was in this sea of thoughts? People, floating immobile in the water, the only sign they were alive their blinking, rolling eyes. A purple haze separated them from their *inamas*, who were anything but immobile. They were thrashing and desperately trying to get back to their people. Whines and howls and all manner of animal sounds rent the air, but no-one could hear them. And there, at the very bottom of the deepest trench, lay Tau. Next to her, on the other side of the barrier, was Nevadra, Tau's *inama.* Nevadra was scratching and biting at the magical barrier, trying and trying to get back to Tau. An old red wolf gently restrained the feisty young lioness with a paw, and smiled ruefully.

"It's no use, you know. Believe me, I've tried. I guess you've just come." A brown hare hopped up to the old wolf's side.

"Hayley?"

"Yes, Lily?"

"I think I might have found a way out!"

Nevadra's eyes widened. "A way to our people?" she asked excitedly.

"Yes, I think so."

"Can you show me, please?"

Lily the hare hopped away, and Nevadra, curious and excited, bounded quickly after her. They came to a small part of the barrier that had a tiny gap. Lily hopped straight through it, and, just as it was about to close, Nevadra struggled through.

Ahead, she saw Lily bounding towards a boy with dark hair and bright green eyes. She woke him, and he stretched, carefully exercising his aching joints and long-stilled muscles. The strange boy got up and walked up out of the water of thoughts, as though on an invisible staircase, Lily bounding happily after him.

Nevadra tore her eyes away from this joyful scene and began to search gingerly-she did not want to step on anyone-among the bodies. She quickly found Tau and gently tried to wake her.

"Tau………Tau, wake up! It's Nevadra!"

At first, nothing happened. Then Tau yawned and stretched.

Wriggling a little, she murmured "Nevadra? But you were……" her voice trailed off. Then Tau leapt up and hugged Nevadra tightly round the middle.

"I knew you would come back to me!"

"Do you think I could go back inside you, please? After all, that is where I belong."

"I don't know if that could actually happen, do you think we could ask Aleesa when we get home?"

"Probably." Nevadra was looking sadly around at the poor souls – literally - still trapped behind the violet barrier.

Tau looked confused. "Wait a sec, how on earth are we supposed to get out of here, Nevadra?"

"What? Oh, it's easy. Feel beneath your feet and you'll hopefully find a staircase."

Tau poked around with her toes and found, to her surprise, a sturdy, rocky step. She looked down and there was nothing there.

"Um, Nevadra, are you *absolutely* sure?"

Nevadra frowned. "Can't you see them? Well then, just feel with your toes."

So Tau gingerly stepped up onto the first invisible step and felt around, wobbling on one leg, searched for the next step. She only found it, though, when she stubbed her toe on thin air.

Quickly stepping up, encouraged that she now had Nevadra beside her, Tau made it up the invisible staircase, without stubbing any more of her toes. And as her head broke the surface of the thoughts, her mind returned to consciousness.

Chapter Eight

She Walks Beside You

Tau opened her eyes and suddenly everything hurt. Her chest ached, her arms were stiff, even the roots of her *hair* hurt. She carefully swivelled her neck. Ouch. It had clicked. Looking down at her chest, she saw that there were no bandages covering it. The wound had healed up and was not infected, but there were deep, red scars all around it from the strange black webbing. Slowly and, very carefully, she turned her head round. Lioness was curled up on the pillow next to her. When the cat noticed that Tau was watching her, she stopped trying to get to sleep and purred,

"How are you? You've been out for simply ages!" Lioness wasn't cross with Tau, she was just concerned about her.

"Where's Nevadra?" Tau croaked, her throat parched.

"Your *inama*? She can't go back inside you, that isn't possible, so for now she's under your bed. She walks beside you now."

"Under my-"

Just then, Darlene came up the stairs and entered the room. Lioness was immediately silent.

"You're up!" Darlene exclaimed delightedly. The floor creaked as she rushed over to the bed.

"Uh, hi, Mum." croaked Tau, "I think my chest's healed up." *Please don't look under the bed… Please, please don't look under the bed……* thought Tau.

Instead of bustling about the room and checking under and on top of everything, Darlene looked concerned,

"You haven't had any water for days. I'll just go and get you a glass." The door creaked a little as she opened it. As soon as

Darlene's muffled footsteps had faded away, Lioness started talking again.

"Yes, under your bed. And if you want proof, you can see her for yourself. Nevadra, can you come out?"

The young lioness slunk out from under the bed, looking thin and tired. She smiled - showing her sharp canines - when she saw Tau. Nevadra said, "Do you remember when you were in Suspension?"

Tau shivered. "Don't remind me." She spoke quietly.

"Did you see me?"

"Yes! Yes, I saw you, but I couldn't get to you! And it felt terrible not being able to move, and not being able to touch you or reach out to you. I tried and tried to get to you, but you weren't responding. I think that violet barrier had something to do with it. It was blocking our attempts to communicate!"

" Breathe. Be careful, Tau, don't over-exert yourself, you don't want to lose the little health you've earned, do you?"

Tau thought about carrying on with her rant, but she was beginning to feel tired already, so she answered, "No, I probably don't, so I'll stop." Tau closed her eyes and lay back on the pillow, breathing heavily.

"You know," said Nevadra, "I don't think that barrier should be there at all. Suspension should be a happy place, where people and *inamas* alike can share thoughts and become friends. That barrier is blocking all attempts for an *inama* and its person to communicate with each other. I don't even think it was there when Suspension was created."

Just then, Nevadra noticed that Saqqara was waiting outside the window, obviously for news of Tau's condition. He saw her looking at him and frowned, concentrating hard. A moment later, an image of Tau lying on her bed with a question mark hovering over her head appeared in Nevadra's head; it meant: "How is she?"

Nevadra thought for a moment, then sent back an image of Tau sitting up in bed and smiling, with Saqqara sitting beside her; it meant:

"She is alive and well, and she wants to see you."

And with that, Saqqara leapt straight through the window, clearing the sill and the frame, and landed rather *too* lightly upon the floorboards, and even so, the wooden boards still creaked. Everyone jumped a little as he landed. In fact, Aleesa panicked, exploded into grains of sand, and fell through the floorboards. Immediately, there came an angry shout from below.

"Tau! What on earth is happening up there? A load of sand just fell through the ceiling and a woman appeared out of nowhere!"

Feigning cheerfulness, Tau called back.

"Oh, its probably just a figment of your imagination, Mum."

No sound came from downstairs. A cloud of sand rose up through the floor and Aleesa materialised in front of them. Her hair was mussed and flew everywhere, like an approaching sandstorm.

"She saw me!" Aleesa whispered, eyes wild and terrified.

"The One Beings are secret. We *must not* be seen!"

Tau straightened.

"*We?* There's more than one of you?"

"Of course! Surely you didn't think that *I* am the only One Being in *the whole world?*"

Tau looked sheepish. "Well, um……….. yes I did. Anyway,

Are there any *men* One Beings?"

Aleesa laughed. "*Men*! Men lack the proper care and commitment to be One Beings and would be distracted and side tracked by *supposedly* better things. A woman's maternal instincts allow her to care."

"What about the other One Beings?"

Aleesa thought for a moment. "Well, there's Carmine, the One Being of fire and heat. She can be very feisty at times, but she's extremely protective of her friends. She knows the crackle and hiss of every fire. Then there's Fern, the One Being of all nature and plants. She's very caring and loving, but can sometimes get very angry. She can talk to vines, animals and flowers. Fern once had a very interesting argument with a bee. Something to do with the bee in question eating more than its share of honey, I believe. After her there's Athena, the One Being of the movements of the air and weather. She hears the shouts of the storms and the whispers of the winds." Then a look passed over her face, almost like pure happiness.

"And dear Addie."

Tau was confused. "Addie?"

Aleesa smiled. "She hates it when I call her that, but we're still best friends. I should call her Adelaide. She's the One Being of oceans and rivers. She can understand the sayings of the sea spray and the ramblings of every river."

"And Amala, the Lady of the Moon?" asked Tau.

Aleesa was still thinking. Finally, she seemed to hit upon something.

"Wait a second, wait a second, there's one more One Being I need to tell you about. Liana, the One Being of stone and rock.

Now, when *she* gets cross, it's a sight to see. Just imagine it! Rockslides rolling down the mountainsides, earthquakes just waiting to topple you off your feet and swallow you up, the ground ripping and splitting apart below you, the rumbling and clattering of the tumbling stones and cracking and quaking ground! It might have been scary, but it was awesome!"

Tau shivered a little. "I think I would be better just imagining it, thank you." A light chuckle passed Aleesa's lips and her eyes twinkled.

"What about Amala?" Tau prompted.

"The Lady? She is very beautiful, with long, black, star-spangled hair, and pale, almost white skin, and the brightest indigo eyes, with a star in their depths, like mine. One of her eyes is known as the North Star."

Tau gasped. "You mean she *is* the sky?"

"Yes; her hair sort of reaches round one side of the Earth and it's night time on that side of the world-"

Tau was excited now. "Why does her eye *never move*?"

Aleesa smiled and a mischievous spark ignited in both her eyes.

"Oh," she said, "it's not her eye that stays still."

Tau looked flabbergasted; all the things she had ever learnt in the few astronomy lessons she had had in her life had just gone down the drain in that one sentence.

Aleesa seemed to snap out of some trance of thought. "But enough of that," Aleesa waved her hand dismissively in the air, "I came for another reason, Tau Oyenusi. I came to tell you something you would have never known if I weren't here. You are the eldest of the Armeni." She repeated the sentence twice more, and she didn't say it, she sang it, making stronger than just a line of words; making it something binding, a charm, a chain of letters.

Tau blinked. "The eldest of the *what*?" But she had felt the tingle in her veins when Aleesa had uttered that word. *The Armeni.*

"You don't know the name? Oh, of course you don't, only a One Being could have told you that. The Armeni are the children of the Sea of Night and types of animals from all around the world. I am going to tell you your life story, Tau."

Chapter Nine

Rage and Power

"I knew you were born the moment you were, as One Beings can sense things like that, but imagine my surprise when I found not a screaming baby but a twelve-year-old girl! When I found you, sitting on a thin crust of rock in the Earth's core-"

"What! *The Earth's core*?" Tau screeched incredulously.

Aleesa put her head in her hands. "Yes *the Earth's core*. Armeni can survive the heat and the magma because that's where they're *born,* so it's *obvious* that they are impervious to it otherwise they would *die ten seconds* after being born! Anyway, you were sitting on that bit of rock, staring at your hands, which had spirals of sand swirling up from them. You waved them a little, and a wisp of it floated up into the heat-charged air and I made it larger and larger until I formed it into the shape of a lioness and made it bound around in the air above you, and you laughed, and it was a child's laugh, and it sounded strange coming out of the mouth of a young woman. Then, you flicked your hand the tiniest amount and the sand lioness leapt down and curled up beside you. You stroked it and placed your hand on its neck and it was *alive*."

At this point, Nevadra spoke up. "That was *me*, I remember it. *You* created me, Tau."

Tau, by now, was extremely confused. "But I'm *normal*. Darlene is my *mother*. I don't remember *any* of it."

Aleesa paled visibly. "I have dreaded telling you this, Tau, all my long, long life." She shivered. "I-I was scared that Mejia would find out that a new magical being had been created in case she used you - so I-I gave you a memory wipe-"

For a moment, Tau's face registered only blank shock, then her look became furious. "You," she growled through clenched teeth,

"You deprived me of my rightful memories and, by extension, my own life." Tau's hands began to pulse with punishing savannah heat. A wisp of white-hot sand rose from her palms and dissipated into the heat haze fast forming above Tau's fingers.

"You-you d-don't understand-" whispered Aleesa, clearly traumatised at the reaction she had caused.

"Yes I do." Tau's growling whisper was layered with rage and filled with ferocity. "You wanted me to never know who I was, where I came from, what I could do. You lied to me. But, most of all, you wanted me to never feel the wonderful sensation of *burning someone's face into a tiny mound of cinders.*"

Tau climbed out of her bed and advanced towards Aleesa, hands as hot as Timbavati in the middle of the dry season, the heat haze it caused blurring her visage. She raised her palms, and heat blasted across the room.

"There!" Aleesa pointed triumphantly

to Tau's hands.

Tau started, but did not stop walking forward. She started to form a question, but, before she could finish it, Aleesa overruled her.

"Wha-"

"You are magical! Look what you can *do*! The thread of your life is intricately entwined in the fabric of Africa indeed. Tau, *please* don't burn me just yet, there's one more thing I need to tell you. Saqqara, listen as well." She took a deep breath. "Your mother, Tau, the lioness Ida, had another child, a lion. You and Saqqara are siblings."

A twin roar of incredulous confusion emanated from both Tau and Saqqara's throats. Then the burning glare returned to both of Tau's eyes and she continued walking forward. Without a word or sign of warning, Saqqara leapt forward and grabbed Tau in his jaws by the scruff of her neck and shook her like she was no more than a rag doll, before carrying her over to the bed as if she were only a cub, and replacing her firmly back in it. Tau wriggled, squirmed and kicked, and managed to smack Saqqara right on the nose, leaving a smoking burn. She also tried to get back out of her bed, her still-hot hands burning through the covers, but suddenly the glare faded from Tau's eyes and she fell back, seemingly drained, onto the mattress. She blinked, and stared around the room. A look of confusion came over her face. Tau opened her mouth and said,

"What did I do?"

Chapter Ten

The Influence of Mejia

"You don't know what you did?" growled Saqqara. "You burned me, tried to kill Aleesa, and scared us all to death to boot!"

"Did I? I am sorry, Elder Brother."

"As am I, Little Sister."

In an urgent tone, Aleesa asked "Tau, what did it *feel* like?"

Brow furrowed in concentration, Tau answered "It felt like...........like a sheet of freezing ice had been placed over my mind, so I couldn't reach it, and I couldn't reach out to you, Nevadra, either. Then it felt like someone had sort of *delved* into my head and replaced my mind with their own, then, there was nothing in my head except an empty, numb, icy wasteland. Then I must have started doing the things you said I did."

Aleesa's lips tightened and her teeth clenched, her eyes blazing. "Mejia." she muttered. "I knew it. She always uses her 'icy wasteland' technique."

Tau, and everyone else in the room, flinched a little at the name.

Aleesa looked bitter, for a moment Tau could almost see the old, old woman behind that beautiful, ageless exterior. A rueful smile crossed her lips.

"Would you like to know the truth, Tau?"

"The truth? The truth has caused me many problems in the past, yet I find it reassuring to know what is happening in reality," conceded Tau.

"Would you like to know the truth about me?"

"But you've already told me."

"Not all of it." Aleesa looked mournful, even ashamed.

"I had foster parents, like you, and

when I started to show my powers, I was in a rage, and because I am a One Being my powers are much stronger than yours, and I managed to swamp the entire house in sand. My foster parents either were crushed under the weight or suffocated. I had a foster sister as well, Jemima. She escaped, I think." Her eyes became old and sad again, her hair lank, her dress unmoving. For a moment, she was silent, then a great, howling wail of despair and hurt passed her lips. Suddenly, there came the thumping of Darlene's slippered feet on the dusty stairs.

The footsteps came closer.

Aleesa whispered "*Salient, turncund.*"

When they had faded away completely, Aleesa explained what she had done was a small memory replacement spell to convince Darlene it had been nothing.

"Now, Tau." Aleesa looked at the dark-haired girl, resting her head in her hands. "Do you *feel different?*"

Chapter Eleven

Becoming

Tau felt very strange indeed. A heat haze was forming above her hands again and her eyes sparkled bright amber. Her canines grew longer and sharper and a long stripe of silky, sandy hair lined the underside of her black locks. A gentle growl issued from her mouth. Her eyes slanted and became more feline, her pupils pointed at both ends and oval-like in the middle. Sand swirled around Tau like a tornado, before engulfing her. After a couple of minutes, it receded. For a moment, Tau was naked, but then sand swirled around her for a second time, forming her a dress like Aleesa's. She stared down at herself, then said "I don't like dresses."

Immediately, the dress reformed into a long-sleeved top and leggings. Tau smiled. ''That's better." The clothes still swirled, but were solid yet flexible.

Aleesa smiled. "Armeni, becoming complete."

Tau continued staring at herself in the mirror stand on her bedside table. "I…I'm different…more lion-like..." She felt gently inside her mouth and stroked her hair. "How did this happen, Aleesa?"

"It is normal for one of the Armeni to Become when they are twelve years of age. You were born *looking* twelve, but, though you were a young woman on the outside, on the inside you were just a child. Because of this, I had to give you and Darlene a completely fresh set of memories. In Darlene's head, you turned up as a baby outside the door and have lived here for the past twelve years, while in reality, you turned up looking twelve but were only a child, a baby. Tau, you have *never aged.* Nothing like this has ever happened in the history of the

Armeni. You are well on the way to being one of the Armelnien. The Special Ones. They are just as normal as other Armeni, but are more One Being-like than any other Armeni. They can *control* the elements of the countries they come from, and Become more animal-like than other Armeni."

Just then, plants enveloped one of the walls, crackling flame the opposite, and a great, shimmering, azure wave another. A cliff of cracked, rugged granite covered the last wall. Wild, howling winds whipped the landscape outside the window.

A whisper of multiple voices flooded around the room. *We know……we know……we know……*

As it faded away, the fire and water and vines receded from the walls and whine of the wind faded from the air, Tau (and everyone else in the room except Aleesa) stared. Lioness's mouth fell open in shock. "What in the wonky world was *that*?"

"It was the other One Beings telling us they know that a new Armelnien has had her Becoming. Wait a second, I need to send a message back."

Chapter Twelve

Idurna Idarya

Suddenly, a darkness came over the room. Then a great light blasted their retinas. The room rippled and changed and changed again, until it finally settled into a shade of grey. Then a voice emanated from the greyness; a whispering voice, a shouting voice, a light and dark voice, a harsh voice of anger, a gentle voice of kindness. "Tau Tionesta. I hear you, I see you, I feel your mind. I am Idurna Idarya, the lost seventh One Being. I am the One Being of life and death, light and darkness."

A small gasp escaped Aleesa, and Tau

frowned a little.

"You call me Tionesta, One Who Mine Eyes Cannot See. That is not my name, for it is Oyenusi."

"Be not confused, Tionesta. You are new to the Eldertongue. It is your Name, meaning She Who is Sired of The Lioness. Your mother, Ida, was as sleek, as gentle and as skilled as any lioness I've known, and more."

"What happened to my mother, Idurna Idarya, Great Ghost of Life and Death?"

"Your mother was swift and beautiful still, but she was old, and a few years ago, a group of hunters shot her. The hunter who performed the deed looked about fifteen, with brown hair and……greyish-yellow eyes. She was in great pain before she died, Tau. I had to take it, to give your mother her rightful peace."

Tau gasped audibly. *It was the same boy,* she thought, *it was the same boy who tried - or maybe accidentally tried - to kill me killed my mother.*

The voice became gentle and sympathetic, but at the same time hard and cold. "Tau, she was tired of life, and I had to take it. She wanted the next world."

Tau was silent and sad. *I did not know my mother; I did not know the person who gave birth to me, raised me.*

"Oh She Who Mine Eyes Cannot See, may I see you?"

"Aleesa, One Being of the Great Continent of Africa, you are young and curious, and this feat requires great energy, but I shall do it."

The darkness and the light came again, and all of a sudden a woman appeared in the room. She was tall and pale, and her body was young, but she walked bent over, with a knotty oaken branch. Old and young at the same time. She seemed to be clothed in light and darkness that was forever rippling and changing. Her face was covered in a long, black veil that allowed barely any view of her face, except a deep, dark, black eye, peering out from beneath the folds of the veil. But - it wasn't black - it was green, brown, a deep and beautiful blue. Then - amber. Bright, bright amber. So bright that it bored into Tau's soul, and a voice entered her thoughts.

Tau. Tau, you are a strong and, compared to your age, wise girl. You are the One chosen to defeat Mejia, or, as we know her, the Ivelneik, the Evil One.

But-but how shall I do this? I am not trained to do this.

You can't be trained. You can only be prepared.

Then the voice was gone, along with the speaker.

"I heard it too, you know, but what she said was different."

"Me too." said Lioness, echoing Aleesa's statement.

"Me three!" yelled Nevadra, and exploded into peals of laughter.

"Child, do not laugh so loudly, though becoming it is, for it fills me with fear that someone may hear you." chided Saqqara.

Tau suddenly jumped out of her bed. "Aleesa, can you prepare me?"

Blank shock showed in Aleesa's face. "Why, Tau, I am not experienced enough. I don't know how."

You do, whispered the voice of Idurna Idayra. *I told you, and I am telling you.*

For a moment, all was silent, then, Saqqara growled "Are you going to start preparing my sister, or not?"

"Okay, okay. First, Tau, we need to know the limit of your abilities, and what you can do. I need you to make your hand hot again, and I'm going to give you a bit of sand, and I want you to try and heat it until it becomes liquid, and maintain it. Then I will instruct you in what to do next."

Tau did as she asked, hot liquid streaming from her fingers, but, strangely, it did not burn them.

"Yow!" Nevadra tried to shake the drop of molten glass off the end of her paw, but it had already burned into her fur. Without thinking, Tau passed her hand over it and the burn healed up and Nevadra's seamless creamy-yellow fur covered it over, leaving no wound.

Aleesa stared at the healed paw. She whispered "A healer! You are truly special, even among the Special Ones." Aleesa turned back to Tau's hand, now almost completely obscured by the heat haze emanating from it, steaming liquid dropping to the ground, leaving the floorboards sizzling.

"Now, I want you to spin it and spin it and spin it, visualising what you want it to become."

Tau did so, and span it and, slowly, a shining sword materialised in the air in front of her.

She opened her eyes, and gasped. "I did *that*?"

Aleesa looked pleased. "Yup. You did that."

"W-What is it?"

"This?" Aleesa inclined her head towards the sword. "It's made of star-glass, so it will never break, but you can mould it and shape it into whatever you like."

Tau stared critically at the sword. "No…" she muttered. The sword began to meld into itself, becoming liquid again, great chunks of previously solid glass dripping down its sides. In a matter of minutes, the sword had become a sturdy staff, wrought in the shape of a knotty branch, much like Idurna Idarya's. At a touch of Tau's finger, a shining, transparent blade slid out of each end with barely a whisper of glass on glass.

Aleesa stroked the shining, transparent material. "It's beau-"

She stopped, frozen. Everyone else in the room froze with her. Suddenly, ice began creep up the walls, silent and menacing. A single icicle fell from the end of Saqqara's nose, tinkling on the floor. Then, a voice hissed from the ice, much like the other One Beings' messages, but more terrible, more menacing, more *evil.*

I know, Tau Tionesta. I know, and be afraid.

Then the chill receded from Tau's veins, but the room remained frozen. *Aleesa, I speak to you, my sister.* The word *sister* was spat out of the unseen mouth, as though it had a rotten taste. *I have hated you since the moment you were born, and only now do I have a chance to show my hate, for I have power beyond even Amala's reckoning!* Then a great crowing sound echoed around the room, burning the ears and chilling the heart. The terrible laugh faded into the wooden walls, but still everyone in the room except Tau was still, well, still. Then, a curious 'mmmmmmmmming' sound came from the corner of the room. Everyone's eyes turned to the corner and Saqqara was standing, glued to the floor, eyes blazing. Tau listened to his thoughts (a thing she found she had a talent for straight after her Becoming) for a moment, then said "Saqqara, *please* stop swearing in Lion." She walked over and rubbed her newly heated hands over his shivering body, melting the strange mental ice with the power of her hands and her mind. And as soon as he was free, he began to hiss and spit, then finally, he choked out

"I…I'll go to her pride right now, and tear them to pieces!"

As Tau freed Aleesa, Aleesa looked sadly at Saqqara. "She has no pride, Saqqara. She has long abandoned the company of humans and………..those she sees as normal. She prefers - or maybe has to prefer - the company of the demon who took control of her."

"A demon?" Tau gasped, and as she was in the middle of freeing Lioness, she almost burned her.

When everyone was free, Aleesa began to explain.

"When the world was young, Mejia tried to create an iron ring, in order to take control of the demon which she had trapped inside it. She spent ages forging it, and when it was ready, she tried to put it on, but instead of sliding onto her finger, it flowed over the whole of it. The creature flooded into Mejia's mind and, well, took control of her. The demon bleached out everything that made her herself, the colour of her hair, the personality of her soul. If someone could cut off her finger(if you touch it, it would take control of *you*) then she would become herself again."

Tau looked down at her staff, which had frozen in her hand when Mejia had spoken to them, and about two seconds later, the staff shattered, a dark fungus festering in its heart. Aleesa noticed this, and yelled "Get away from that!" and pushed them all to the opposite wall.

The black fungus spread at abnormal speed, and it didn't look like a fungus anymore, more like a *darkness*, spreading and spreading through the star-glass staff, the fragments knitting together to create a seamless whole, but just as Tau reached for it, a great roaring, rushing noise came from it and the thing inside it - for it was no longer a fungus, nor a darkness, but a strange *something* that was not gas, nor solid, nor even liquid, but sometimes it resembled a bundle of black worms- and it pinched in, and then exploded outwards into the room, and rushed out of the window, leaving dark, festering spots on the walls, and as they looked on, they burned dark holes into the plaster, which, as they began to get deeper, they began to spread down and across the walls.

"That was a demon, or a part of a demon. It has infected the walls, but if we keep away from them, and the demon travels fast, of which I am sure, they should run out of juice pretty quickly, say, five minutes." Aleesa let them past her outstretched arms.

Even as they watched, the holes stopped spreading, and ground to a halt. Tau stepped forward, and tentatively poked the edge, and it left a small smudge on her finger. She quickly passed her hand over it, and the surface of the pad of her index finger cleared. Then, quite without meaning to, her hand brushed the edge of one the spots. It began to recede and shrink until only clean, white plaster was left behind. This she repeated, until all the walls were clear of blemishes. Aleesa looked at the window, then quickly melted some sand with her hands and repaired it.

Then, suddenly, there came the sound Darlene's footsteps on the stairs. Nevadra dove under the bed, Saqqara ran towards the wardrobe while Aleesa held the door open, before Aleesa herself dissolved into sand. Tau lay down and pretended to be asleep, and Lioness curled up on the pillow. Darlene opened the door and glanced around the room, then looked down.

Somehow, Saqqara managed to nudge the door of the wardrobe, and it creaked open a little. Darlene's head snapped up. She muttered "That door never shut properly anyway," and then she turned and shut the door as she went out. Aleesa materialised in front of them, and Saqqara burst out of the closet. The doors hung down, half off their hinges, and a second later, one of the doors fell completely off its hinges, and landed with a clatter on the floor. Nevadra leapt out from under the bed, and looked at the fallen door. "Saqqara, did you do that?"

Saqqara looked sheepish. "Yes, I did."

Aleesa sighed, and a tendril of sand lengthened out from her hand, picked up the door and replaced it on the hinges of the wardrobe with a click. Then Aleesa turned to Tau. "To unlock the final part of your Armelnien Becoming, you must greet the others of your kind."

"The others? The Armelnien?"

"Yes. Open your mind, young Armelnien. Feel your brothers and feel your sisters."

Tau did as she asked, broadening her mind, and reaching out with it. Suddenly, and without warning, a thousand or more voices filled Tau's mind, and so much unheard sound filled Tau's head that she curled into a ball on the floor. Finally, she managed to blot out all the voices but one, a boy's. At first, he did not notice, but a few seconds later, he did.

Yes, yes, whatever. I don't mind............... Oh. Hello. Are you new to your powers?

Yes. Who are you? What animal are you the Armelnien of?

My name is Kyamaln. I am the Armelnien of the golden eagle. Who are you?

My name is Tau Tionesta. I am Armelnien of the lion. I came to unlock the last of my powers as an Armelnien. Please could you do it for me?

This I grant you, Tau Tionesta. Go, and discover yourself.

Then, the voice was gone.

When Tau opened her eyes, she knew something was different. For a start, she was lower to the ground than usual, and she was receiving far to much sensory information. She could smell the sandy scent of the desert outside, the hot smell of the new glass in the window, the date-sweet perfume of Aleesa. Her hearing was sharper than before, as well. She could hear the creak of the floorboards as Saqqara bent his foreleg, the sandy rustle of Aleesa's swirling dress, the gentle *thump thump* of Lioness's tail on the bed. Then, the voice of Kyamaln sounded in her head again, this time with a touch of amusement. *Young one, you have found yourself. Look down. Look behind yourself.*

Tau looked. Two paws lay on the ground in front of her. She looked behind herself. A creamy tail waved in the air behind her.

Finally, Tau realised. *I'm a lion!*

Chapter Thirteen

We Must Walk

Yes, you are. Aleesa's voice sounded in Tau's head, and she looked across at her. Aleesa was also a lion, but she was larger than Tau. Her tail waved in the air. *Come outside with me. We must walk together. We have much to talk about.*

Together they leapt out of the window, and into the desert. The dry, waving grass surrounded them, and they sheltered behind it to talk, or so Tau thought. Then, the Aleesa-lion padded up to her.

Come. Did I not say I would walk with

you?

Yes, indeed you did, Mistress.

As they walked out from behind the large tuft of savannah grass, Tau almost gasped as the unforgiving desert heat blasted them. But, as she squinted into it, she felt the cooling presence of a shading spell. Tau tried to speak, to ask if she had cast the spell, but all that passed her lips was a growling, hissing sound. But, as Tau heard the sound of her voice, she found she could *understand* it.

This is what came out of her mouth: "Grrrrrrrrrrr-"

But this is what she heard: "Did you ca-"

She never finished her sentence, for at that moment, a shining, golden eagle appeared, shimmering, in the air above her. As she looked at it, she realised she recognised the vast, rippling consciousness that touched hers. She cried out with her mind, *Kyamaln!*

The voice that replied was quieter and more subdued than their first mind-meeting, but still the voice spoke back. *Tionesta. It is good we meet again. You have the full amount of your powers, I see.*

Yes, I do, she replied, *oh, and how good it feels!*

Yes, little one, I should know, for I felt the same when it happened to me.

Tau's thoughts sounded with concern. *But-but why are you here, Kyamaln? The savannah is no place for a golden eagle such as yourself.* Indeed, Kyamaln was shaking and trembling, and it seemed that the heat of the desert was pressing down on him. Tau asked *Are you alright, Kyamaln? Come and get under the shading spell, and after all, you did cast it yourself.* Kyamaln gratefully bobbed his head. *Yes.* He flapped his wings three times and screeched very loudly, then the air rippled and shimmered like a heat haze, and the shimmering air stretched over Kyamaln's eagle form, and arched down on the other side of him, slowly melding into the ground, then the shimmer was gone, fading away up the air and the air became cool and shady again. *Aaah. That's so much better.*

Chapter Fourteen

The Boy

Now that he was inside the safety of the spell, he began to shed his feathers. Slowly, his outline blurred, and he grew taller, his wings receding into his back. Where the eagle had hovered, there now hovered in the air a boy of about seventeen, with brown hair. Then he fell, and landed with a thump on the hard, dry, hot ground of the savannah. A loud, mental *ouch* sounded in Tau's head. Then he lifted his head, and Tau saw the greyish-yellow eyes of the boy who had shot her.

Suddenly, the world swam around her, and almost all of her vision was obscured by blackness, so that all that she could see was a single pinpoint of light; the boy's eyes. Then, she saw no more.

When Tau regained consciousness, she found Aleesa-lion licking her face. Then her outline blurred, and she became her human form again.

"Wake up, Tau! Wake up!"

Tau's head swivelled to one side, and she caught sight of the boy, Kyamaln. His eyes were full of sadness and regret, and then he said, "I am sorry, little one, for all I have done. I-I want you to see your mother-so........." His voice trailed off.

"Come, Tau." Aleesa held out her hand to Tau. She took it, and pulled herself up. Aleesa led her over to a patch of lush grass, that Tau had not seen before. She looked at it with scepticism. It looked just like any other patch of grass to her. Then Aleesa told her to turn back into a lioness again, and Tau was confused. "I don't know how to, I did it last time without thinking it."

"Try, Tau. *Think* that you are a lioness, and you will *be* one. Draw on the Armelneinstal, the magical crystal that resides inside your chest, and *Be.*"

Tau did so, and imagined that she was hunting, her paws padding silently through the grass, lips drawn back in a snarl, showing her teeth. She leapt forward…… Tau landed with a scrabble of claws on the hard, compacted ground of the savannah. Quickly scrambling to her feet again, Tau looked around. Aleesa was standing with her back to her, chanting and passing her hands over the patch of grass. Then, the air shimmered above the grass, much like the shading spell that Kyamaln had cast. It accumulated in one place, bunching together above the patch of grass. Suddenly, in one instant, the air formed the shape of a lioness.

Chapter Fifteen

Ida

She was lean and beautiful, vicious and cunning, motherly and caring. All the things that a lioness should be, and a little more of *something*, a little more......magical. The sleek, yellowish shape of the lioness twisted in the air and looked behind and around herself, her amber eyes opening and shutting. Her tail waved in confusion, and her ears pricked. When she had pivoted around in the air twice, she stared down at Tau. Her eyes blinked open, then shut again, then a voice entered her head.

Tau? Is it you?

Mother? Ida of The Armeni? Yes, it is I, your daughter, Tau Tionesta.

You are Special! I never thought you would, but you did! You did! The voice of Ida was filled with such hope and joy that Tau could not help but smile.

Why do you smile, my daughter?

Tau replied, *I smile only because you are happy, my mother, as am I.*

Iyla ghana arianta yialan. I shall never desert you. Ida spoke in Tau's mind

Netheran, iyla youcalan. Youmayn shakan iamnalwa inma heatanar inma caryana. Neither I you. You shall always be in my heart, my mother. Tau felt strangely heavy, her heels sinking into the sandy ground. Then the voice of Ida was in her head.

I am here, my daughter, inside your heart, and I shall accompany you to The Northern Reaches, and I shall help you however I can in the journey to and fight against Mejia, or as The Lady knows her, Sophia Ionian.

Her name is not Mejia? But how could she have changed her Name? asked Tau.

They were speaking in the Eldertongue, so Tau could not understand *how* Mejia had changed her *ianthulac*, her Name. It was the name that, if spoken by another, would give the one who spoke it command over the one who the speaker named.

Ida explained to Tau. *She used dark magic to warp it into a different shape. That is how she came to have the desire to be stronger, to want more. That was the start of Mejia. The demon warped her in turn, and made her very soul evil. If you can cut off the middle finger of her left hand, she will be cleansed of the demon's marks.*

Quicker than the eye could follow, Tau snapped out a paw, and, completely out of instinct, clenched it tight. As she lifted it, she saw, clenched within it, a small sandfish. It was like a smooth-backed but somehow scaly lizard, with clawed, spreading feet and long head, and jaws, though cute-looking, were full of sharp teeth. Then, an angry, indignant squeak of a voice appeared in her head.

Oi! I'm an Armelnien, you know. My name is Tiala, and, she squirmed her body around to reveal a second, identical head underneath her, *this is my twin sister, Niña.* Then, she squirmed some more, and asked

Can you let me go? I mean, I need to find Tau, the new Armelnien, to greet her, and to advise her on fighting tactics on how to fight Mejia.

Tau almost smiled. *But, Oh Sand-shifting One, I am Tau.*

Then, Oh Newbie, if you will, let me go!

Tau suddenly realised that she, had in her excitement, tightened her claws somewhat around the waist of the sandfish, her claws scratching at her scaly-smooth back. Quickly loosening it, she allowed the little sandfish and her twin sister to scramble out of her large paw.

Then, simultaneously their outlines blurred, and two identical girls, with not dark, but not light coloured skin, but somewhere in the middle appeared. Their hair was reddish-blonde, the light orange colour of the scaly backs of the sandfish, and their eyes were the light yellow, slit-pupiled ones of the small lizards. Their skin seemed dry and a little flaky; reminiscent of the scales of their animal. They had linked arms, and their look was sour. One of them was about three millimetres taller than the other. The taller one spoke, and her voice was not welcoming. "That hurt, you know. *Yiamnta nonmere Mejia kilanman, youmaak notta byana alla friendacompanyona. Thisa iyla swearnaak.* Even if you do defeat Mejia, you will not be one of our closest friends. This I swear."

At the last sentence, the smaller, possibly younger twin, joined in. Then Saqqara loped towards the two of them, and roared in their faces, before batting at them, seemingly without effort, and knocked them down as if they were only a couple of skittles. They landed on their backs with a satisfying *thump* of flesh on ground. Then he roared at them,

"She is my sister, and if you're not nice to her, you'll have *me* to deal with." As they tried to get back up again, he batted them back to the ground, scraping them across the back a little. Though it was only shallow, the younger still winced, though the elder did not seem to notice, even though drops of scarlet blood splattered on the ground.

If he had done it a little harder, and in a different place, it would have broken through their skulls. They scrambled, on their hands and knees, away from him, and were they not trembling too much to speak, they would have been shrieking. They neared the great spire of reddish rock, still on all fours and backed up against it, until they could go no further.

Then, their outlines blurred simultaneously, and the two sandfish skittered down in to the sand. As they disappeared, the squeaky voice came into Tau's head again, this time scared-sounding and higher in pitch than before. *It's going to be alright, Niña, it's going to be alright. We'll never go back to that lion ever, ever again. Do you hear me! Never, ever again. Oh Newbie, we shall never love you, even as a sister in the great family of the Armelnien.*

Tau tried to apologise, but a strong, iron wall guarded the thoughts of Niña and her sister from her apologising thoughts. *Sorry. Sorry! Look, will you listen to me!* But it was to no avail. Tau tried to make a star-glass sword, but they were long gonc. The half-formed sword melted into a stub, the sizzling droplets throwing up a small cloud of sandy dust, and the squeaks of disturbed animals filled the air. Saqqara hung his head. *I didn't like to do that,* he thought at her. *Hurting another Armelnien is punishable by death.*

Who told you that? Tau asked.

Aleesa.

There is much Aleesa does not relate to me, then.

Only the whisper of sand betrayed Aleesa's presence, and her voice floated down to their minds, soft as a summer breeze.

Tau, I will tell you, but all in good time. I am sorry, but the laws of the Armelnien are not of use in the present circumstances. But, you are very, very lucky, Saqqara, that no Armelnien Marshal saw you doing that. They would have had your pelt, they would, beautiful and pale, pure white though it be. They would have had it. One day, Saqqara, do not blame me as I say this, it is not a threat, but one day, you will pay for this. Her voice receded away from their minds, and her words echoed in both of their heads. Saqqara trembled, then spoke, and his voice was like that of a lion cub, if lion cubs could talk. "I-I don't w-want to d-die!"

On the outside, Tau's voice was firm and confident. (On the inside, she too was scared that her own brother would be killed by her own race.) "You will not die, my Brother. *Younaak wolano diethyen.* You will not die." Then she rushed over to Saqqara, and wrapped her arms around his neck, digging her hands into his fur. The voice of her mother sounded in her head *Do not be sad, my daughter, for if he should die, remember that you shall one day join him in the* hapuylandonmuy*, the Land Where Everyone Is Happy. Heaven.*

Tau half-smiled, then, quickly and suddenly, exhaustion and sleep overcame her. She slept in the soft, white, moving mattress of Saqqara's back, gently, deeply sleeping, her chest undulating up and down in unison with Saqqara's furry shoulders.

The last sight she saw before sleep overtook her was the twinkling lights in the purple African sky, the lilac coloured part where the sun had just sunk, the constellation that she had always loved so, the one of a lion's face, the one missing its nose. Then, darkness enveloped her sight, and exhaustion dragged at her limbs, forcing her body into a curled up position, hugging Saqqara's mane. She fell into the dark, gentle embrace of wonderful, blissful sleep.

Chapter Sixteen

Waking with Saqqara

At first light, Tau awoke, and found herself on the ground, but she felt something large, alive and moving breathing beside her, its fur rubbing against her. She felt scared for a moment, then she remembered the last day, and huddled against Saqqara's warm, soft side, warming her veins with his body heat.

He stirred, and moved in his sleep, pushing Tau a foot away from him. Tau shielded her eyes as the sun rose, filling the savannah with light and colour, the dark shadows of night creeping away, colour spreading out across the land like paint across a canvas, filling up the land to the horizon. Saqqara stirred, lifted his head, and blinked blearily in the direction of the newly reborn sun. Then he turned, and he was surrounded by beautiful, shining light, and he was so proud, and so powerful, that she could not help but kneel before him, and declare,

"Oh Beautiful One, I am your servant, and I swear my staff to you."

Saqqara smiled a toothy approximation of a smile, and for a moment, sparkling tears danced in his eyes, then he proclaimed "Oh Golden Sands And Gleaming Staff, arise, and do as you will, for you are my Sister, and we are each others servant, and our bond is that of mutual friendship."

And he took her in his paws, and they danced and rolled and played together until sunset, and they collapsed together, rolling over and over on the ground, so happy, brother and sister together, so happy that Aleesa could barely bring herself to separate them, to teach Tau on the art of swordplay, but, she agreed with herself, it was necessary. She called to her from the house, "Tau! Tau! Come. I have need of you, for it is for you."

Tau broke away from Saqqara, and with a look of such sorrow upon her beautiful face, turned and ran on light feet back to the house, back to Aleesa, back to education; away from the beauty and the wildness and the freedom of the wilds of the savannah.

Aleesa stood there, waiting for her, and as she ran up to her, panting, and said, "Oh Aleesa, One Being of the Great Continent of Africa, why have you called me?"

Aleesa told her to create another staff, like the one which had been destroyed by the demon. And so she did, and the glass moulded and shaped, and soon the shining staff was whole and beautiful again, and the blades slid out of each end with barely a whisper of glass on glass. Then, Aleesa began to instruct her in the arts of swordplay, or, more correctly, *eyldunstafplayagnen*, for that was what the glass staff, was called. The *eyldunstaf.*

Tau perfected this form of weaponry by sparring with Aleesa, because she had one as well, but she could never get the footwork quite correct. Then, she asked to be excused, and went into her room - for they had been sparring outside - and she reached out with her mind to Idurna Idarya. And she answered. *Little Armelnien, what do you want?*

How do you entrust your life to another person?

Reach in to yourself, and take it. And with that question-inducing answer, she was gone.

Tau went outside, and before asking Aleesa her question, she reached inside herself and plucked a ball of life like a flower. She felt the strange substance, neither solid, nor liquid, nor gas. It was not something insubstantial, rather something with a consciousness, something with a driving purpose, to keep its owner alive. Then, she told Aleesa, "Aleesa, would you take care of me? Would, if I was killed by Mejia, would you preserve my life?"

Aleesa did not know what to think, so she talked instead. "This is a great honour, Tau Tionesta, one that you cannot entrust to one so young - by One Being standards, at least - and inexperienced as me."

"I could not trust anyone more, Aleesa, One Being of the Great Continent of Africa. You would do me a great favour, the greatest favour of all favours ever paid, for you will be preserving me."

"But," questioned Aleesa, a frown upon her face, "How should I be able to give you a body?"

"Build a sand-me, and place the ball of life in the centre of the sand-me's chest, and you will see the pigmentation of my skin spread forth from that spot, and then a smaller ball shall rise from my chest, and you shall place it upon my brow. The blue of the life shall spread through my hair, then it shall become darker, and the sandy stripe that lines it shall be there, and I shall look just the same, but you must give me thoughts. Take them, and look after them, and if I should die, do as I have told you, please."

Then, Tau gave her the ball of life, and she saw that Aleesa was weeping. Then, Tau stood tall and rigid, and Aleesa took her most innermost thoughts, the thoughts that made her herself. Aleesa stored them deep within her, and kept them there, so they were safe. Tau bent her head and felt out with her mind for her thoughts. She could still feel them, but where were they? She couldn't find them. She sat on the floor in a heap, and cried, "Where are they? I want them back!"

Chapter Seventeen

Hostile Thoughts

Aleesa knelt beside her distraught form. She reached out with her mind, to calm her, but it was to no avail, for a wall of iron surrounded her mind. Then a dagger of razor-sharp thought plunged into Aleesa's mind. Aleesa felt Tau's angry voice inside her head, but she felt the great and terrible sadness that was underlying it, and she tried to comfort her.

Tau! Be calm, and do not be angry. I took them. Do you not remember?

The dagger came again, and Aleesa's

thoughts were almost torn apart into floating, babbling drifts of madness, but she managed to stop it just in time. She blanketed down on Tau's mind with her own, smothering it, muffling and blunting the dagger.

Stop this Tau! Stop this! You are hurting me!

But it did not stop. The animal part of Tau had finally broken forth. Suddenly, Tau leapt forwards, and, in one fluid movement, a lioness lunged at Aleesa, and began to circle her.

Aleesa was affronted, then she too changed in to a lioness, and began to circle the Tau-lioness. The Aleesa-lioness feinted to the left, and then lunged at the Tau-lion's face. She caught her on the eye, and a great, bloody gash appeared in the Tau-lion's eyeball. Saqqara, though he was far away, spotted the clouds of dust, and ran to help. When he saw what the Aleesa-lion had done, however, he lunged at her, claws out and teeth bared. But the Aleesa-lion simply flicked her left forepaw, and a great, yellow wall of sand rose up, and no matter what he tried, Saqqara could not break through it. A thin skein of dusky, sand-filled light stretched from Aleesa's body, fortifying the wall and allowing her to combat Tau at the same time.

I told you to stop this, Tau! Restrain yourself, and see the light!

The storm whirling around Aleesa subsided, but a great energy was building in the void it had left behind, and Aleesa knew that Tau - or what was left of her - would not be able to contain it for much longer. A voice emanated from the void, a voice that, though soft, told uncontrollable malice and revenge.

Where is this light, One Who Attacks? For I am surrounded by this oppressing darkness, and cannot see.

Gosh, Aleesa thought, *she has even forgotten who I am.* Then she addressed the Tau-lion.

I am the light. Follow me.

Aleesa sensed a feeling of confusion, then hot, boiling anger, from the void.

Why should I believe one who has attacked me? You would kill me at the first chance you got.

Your reasons are well made and well put, but they are not true. Do you want your memories, Tau?

You call me Tau. That is not my name. I have never had a name, and have never wanted one.

Suddenly, the great energy exploded outwards, and it smothered and whirled around Aleesa's thoughts, and she cried out a piercing, shrieking mental scream, and burned the Tau-lion's eardrums. She withdrew the energy for the second time, and the scream receded.

Then give me my memories, One Who Attacks!

I will. Aleesa-lion walked over to where the Tau lay hunched and shivering upon the ground, her long legs and arms - for she had turned human again - wrapped around her body. She placed her paws upon Tau's breast, and she searched through her entire being, and found the place where she had hidden them. She took them out, and, very gently, made Tau go to sleep, and while she was dozing, she channelled Tau's memories out of her own body, and they were replaced in Tau's brain. She did it while she was asleep because it hurt, as so many memories were bonding with so many others.

Despite her efforts, Tau still moaned and shifted a little in her sleep. At first, Tau's head tried to reject the unfamiliar memories, saying they were not her own, but, gradually, her mind accepted them, but only when she had convinced Tau's mind that they *did* belong there by linking them with other memories.

Tau jerked awake, only to fall back onto the ground with a moan of tiredness. "Uhhhhh……"

Then she snapped back up again, so quickly that Aleesa jumped back a little.

"I remember *everything*!" Tau exclaimed, her eyes bright and joyful.

"The heat of the Earth's core, the joy I felt when I made Nevadra. *Everything*."

"Do you like it?" asked Aleesa from the shade of a scrubby tree.

Tau started, and turned around quickly, then relaxed as she saw Aleesa. Then she realised that one her eyes was red and painful, and tried to blink the redness out, but it would not go away. Aleesa offered her a small star-glass mirror so she could see her wound. When she saw her eye, she gasped with pain and surprise.

"Would you like me to deal with that?" Aleesa loped over as if she had all the time in the world.

"No, I can do it." Tau pressed her

hand over her eye, and held it there for several minutes. When she took it off her eye, it was quite unblemished, except for a long scar along its length.

"Can you see out of that?" Aleesa asked. "Let me have a look."

Tau opened her mind, and allowed Aleesa to see out of her eyes. When she had finished, she stared at Tau, and admiration flooded her face. "Tau, you have done amazingly well, though you may never be able to see as well as you have. It is lucky that I did not scratch you that deeply, otherwise you might be blind in one eye."

Then Tau blinked, and a small rivulet of her blood leaked out of the corner of her eye, and she yelled at the sting of it.

"There now! Look what you've done. I told you to let me look at it." She walked over, and placed her hand over it, just like Tau had done, and chanted "*Omo lana kiyampa, enya helios.*"

She took her hand away, and Tau blinked once. Apart from the scar along its length, her eye was quite seamless and clean. Then she ran around the perimeter of the house, shrieking and screaming with joy.

Then, as she returned to that spot, she noticed that Aleesa was bowed over, as if she was tired. She saw the strange, dusky light that emanated from her body. As her sight panned around, she noticed the wall that prevented Saqqara from reaching her.

Quickly, she ran to Aleesa, slapping her hard around the face, so breaking her concentration and letting the wall tumble to the ground. Saqqara leapt out from behind it, looked a little surprised when his claws hit nothing, then growled, and rushed to attack Aleesa. Tau ran forward, and shouted with her mind: *Stop, my Brother, and end this madness!* Only a terrible, empty wasteland of fear presented itself to her. So Tau, scared that he would kill Aleesa, lunged at Saqqara, and sank her newly-made-sharp teeth into his shoulder, so deep that it almost pierced the muscles in his shoulder. Saqqara swerved around, and growled at Tau, then looked over at his shoulder, then he knelt, and growled in his rough voice, "I hear you, my Sister. I hear you."

In the sudden lull, the window of the house opened, and a cat and a lioness leapt, in perfect sync, out of the window and over the windowsill and onto the sand. Nevadra was panting, her tongue lolling out of her mouth, and her eyes were wild, and Lioness's head was lowered in exhaustion, and their legs were trembling, for the size of the leap they had taken, coupled with the running and talking they had done during the past few hours had left them close to collapse.

They fell onto the sand, and lay there, panting and wheezing until Tau and Aleesa were forced to transfer energy from their own bodies into Lioness's and Nevadra's just to give them the strength to speak. Lioness's head whirled from side to side, and she meowed, "What happened? What happened? What happened?"

Afraid that the cat might start hyperventilating, Tau said, " We're all fine, Lioness. Get u-" Tau's speech was interrupted as a sudden flapping distracted her. She looked around, and caught sight of Kyamaln, in his boy form, standing silent and sad, at the edge of her vision in the shade of the trees by the edge of the house. He came a step closer, and his form was flooded with light. At that moment he looked so beautiful and so amazing that something was released inside Tau, and she felt something she had only ever felt towards Darlene: love. She loved him with all her heart. And she wanted him, she longed for him. It was as Darlene had once said to her; love was The Longing Feeling.

Chapter Eighteen

The Longing Feeling

The world was different. Everything was brighter and more focused. It was like when Tau had had her Becoming, only this it was not a transformation, more like a *revelation.* Now that she was happy, she could sense the happiness of everything around her, like bright stars in a world of darkness.

She could sense the primitive happiness of the plant next to her, because it was nearly the beginning of the wet season, the bright relief-like happiness of Lioness and Nevadra because Aleesa and Tau had made them strong again. And, brightest and most prominent of all, was the happiness of

Kyamaln, who loved her as she did him. And, she thought, it was strange that she loved him, because it was he who had shot her, and shot and killed her mother. So she went over to him, and they met in the shadows of the trees by the house, and, although she had originally come to him with a question in mind, she suddenly found herself kissing him, and it felt so good and so wonderful that she did not break contact. Then she realised that everything around her had gone quiet, and she looked around in curiosity.

Everyone was staring at her; Lioness's mouth was hanging open in surprise; disbelief showed clear in Aleesa's face; Saqqara's great tooth-filled maw opened in a disbelieving growl. But nothing showed on Nevadra's face but passion and love, for the link that bound them together extended far beyond the reaches of speech. Nevadra smiled, and she felt the passion and the longing and the love that Tau was feeling more than anyone else.

Are you loving someone, Tau? asked Ida.

Yes, my mother, and ,oh, how good it feels!

I am happy for you, my daughter.

She was gone.

And as they lay in the shade of the

trees, almost oblivious to all else, they were as happy as anyone could be. Then Nevadra ran over to them, and they curled up and rolled and romped together, in a ball of fierce happiness, rolled over and over until, quite without meaning to, they reached the place where Aleesa, Saqqara, and Lioness were standing. They unrolled, and stood. Tau blushed, and was rather glad it would not show. Then Kyamaln was kissing her again, and she him, and she was totally absorbed, and the only thing that was bothering her was a tiny whisper at the back of her mind; the fact that everyone was watching. Saqqara stepped forward. "I thought you loved me, Tau. I thought you loved *me*."

Tau was troubled for some minutes, and then spoke. "*Iyna doana lovien youana asai onedana friendacompanyona; asai a companyonamaleon. Kyamaln* I do love you, as one of my closest friends; as a brother. Kyamaln loves me as a loved one."

Saqqara growled, "Grrrrrrrr…… I shall fight him for the ownership of the female. Without magic, mind, you tiny little worm. You're not going to fly away, are you?"

Kyamaln nodded, and swore in the Eldertongue, "*Iyla swearnaak thatal iylasaak flinaag awana freom youana durin theen fightaconflictan.* I swear that I shall not fly away from you during the fight. But I shall only do this on one condition, that I may be able to fight in my eagle form. I also have a question. Will this battle be fought mentally or physically?"

Saqqara considered the consequences of both, then, in a burst of rash disregard and pride, growled, "Both. Let it start now."

At that moment, and with no warning at all, Kyamaln leapt forwards, both with his mind and his body. In mid-air, he transformed into an eagle, and flew straight towards Saqqara's face, shining, pointed talons unsheathed, and scratched at his face, bloodying his nose, then lashed out with his mind, and enclosed Saqqara's mind in a whirling storm of darkness.

Saqqara tried to do the same to Kyamaln, but his mind was huge and powerful and mysterious, and so beautiful that anyone normal would have become lost in its depths, subdued by the peaceful, melancholy strains of music that emanated from its centre. Saqqara shied away from the contact, but could not stop it. The strange sea of thought that raged and stormed and wailed like the sea, battering down Saqqara's mental defences, and roaring and shouting inside Saqqara's mind, *Tau is mine! Do you hear me? My own!*

No! She is my sister! My sist-

Outside the whirling tirade of mind on mind, Kyamaln was sitting on the ground, his talons digging into the dirt. He was staring intently at Saqqara, quite calm, as if he was meditating. In stark contrast, Saqqara was lying on the ground, thrashing and growling and yowling, as if in pain, though no mark showed upon his pale fur apart from the scratches that Kyamaln had inflicted. Finally, Saqqara was still, and defeat showed in his white face.

"I submit." He ground out the sentence through clenched teeth. "You are truly stronger than me, and deserve her."

Kyamaln stopped his intense stare, and then busied himself cleaning his talons, which were stained with gore from the scratches he had made on Saqqara's face. Tau rushed forward, and embraced Kyamaln, before whispering to him, "Can I tend to Saqqara's wounds, Kyamaln?"

"Yes, Tau." For a moment more, they embraced each other, then Tau rushed over to Saqqara, and held his face. Blood - Saqqara's blood - stained her palms for a second, then Saqqara's creamy, pale fur flowed over his face like a blanket over a mattress, and was once again unbroken, as if it had never been marred, except for the nasty whitish-reddish mark on his nose, the place where Tau had burned him. When Tau had finished, Saqqara instinctively reached up to scratch his face, but, with a firm hand and stern word, she restrained his paws. "Do you want me to do it all again?"

"No. It itched like crazy."

"Well then, please don't scratch until I tell you to."

As Tau returned to the place where Kyamaln was standing, she asked him, "When you accidentally shot me, after I woke up, Lioness told me one of the hunters called you Jonathan. Why in the wonky world did you change your name?"

"Kyamaln sounds more than a little foreign, don't you think? I had to change my name to something more......*common*."

"Hmm."

"I have a friend - just a friend, no boy or girl involved - you know, called Darla. She's clever and crazy in equal measure, with bright pink hair – don't ask me why - and bright green eyes. Her Armelnien animal is a green gecko. If you plan to travel to the Arctic to combat Mejia, then she lives somewhere in......somewhere. She could be here right know, listening. She *always* seems to be where something of note is happening."

Chapter Nineteen

Darla

Then a strange consciousness touched theirs, but it was not of the menacing kind, rather a laughing, jumping-with-joy kind of a consciousness. A voice entered their thoughts; a strange voice, as has been said, but the kind of voice that Tau associated with 'good'. It was a kind of optimistic voice, the sort you would give a person who was sort of weird, but kind and nice at the same time.

The character the voice implied, at first glance, would be of no use in battle, but if you were to delve deeper, you would find a tongue of smooth steel, adept at worming its way into minds and conversations, and, if combined with magical words, would be able to charm and wheedle an enemy to do whatever the owner of the tongue told them to.

Hello, Kyamaln. Yes, you are correct; I always am there when anything of note is happening.

Darla?

The voice grew slightly annoyed. *Who did you think it was, dunderhead?*

Kyamaln's pride smarted for a moment, then he became composed and smooth again. *There is no need for insults, Darla. Come, and look who is here.*

Darla searched for a moment with her mind, found Tau, read her intentions as easily as if her mind were an open book, and said,

Do you really mean to take up the mantle of the Armelneinconflicanya, *the Armelnien who fought for us?*

I did not know there was any such thing, Friend of Kyamaln. But if you mean I shall engage Mejia in combat, then yes.

And you so young, Tau Tionesta. Humph. You are probably the result of a bet.

As Darla had sifted through her mind, Tau returned the compliment.

And you *betting as well, Friend of He Who Holds My Heart?*

Humph. It was only once, she retorted.

Kyamaln saw the danger of mental combat, so he acted as a peacemaker.

Ladies, ladies, let us have no arguments, please.

He's right, you know, Tau told Darla, *we should not argue among ourselves at this crucial time. Now is the time to make allies, not enemies.*

In a grudging voice, Darla replied, *Yes, you are correct, I suppose.*

Now, show yourself, Friend of Kyamaln.

I am here!

The sand next to Tau's left foot rippled, as it had when the sandfish had appeared, and a small, bright green head, roughly the same shape as the sandfish, and a green, whipping tail were revealed. The bright blur of the tail brushed away the sand from a long body, half-webbed claws, and a bright, intelligent eye.

The gecko wormed its way out of the sand, and, like the rest of the Armelnien that Tau had met in the past few hours (much to her surprise) her outline blurred, and a woman of about middling size materialised in front of them.

She had bright pink hair, as Kyamaln had said, and bright green eyes with the slit pupils of a reptile, reminiscent of her animal form. She had a joyful, optimistic face, and she looked like someone who enjoyed fun and being fun. Darla was wearing a rainbow-coloured spotty top and blue jeans. She was a little bit......*different.*

Darla was not short, but she was rather stocky, and the muscles on her forearms were rather larger and wider than Tau had ever seen on most women before. Darla caught her staring at her arms, and told her, "My father was an English smith. I was his apprentice for a time, but he managed to hit me very hard with his hammer when I accidentally transformed in the middle of the forge. When I turned human again, he took me to hospital, though I have had a scar on my back ever since." She twisted around, lifting up her top. A large, thick scar marred her skin. It was deep, and dark red in colour, with pink, puckered skin around the edges of the roughly circular scar. The folds of her top fell across the scar as quickly as it had lifted. She twisted back around again.

"Oh, and by the way," Darla chuckled, "Father was very surprised when I had my Becoming."

She smiled ruefully at the memory.

Chapter Twenty

Discovery

Just then, a few metres away, the window of Tau's bedroom opened, and Darlene's head poked out. She stared, and saw Saqqara, Lioness, Nevadra, Kyamaln and Darla all at once. She screeched, "Tau! What in the wonky world is going on? Who are these people? Has the-"

Aleesa stepped forward smooth and composed.

"Darlene Tionesta. I am very sorry to tell you this, but Tau is not your child."

She said this with such bluntness, and no softening the huge emotional blow, that no-one could expect Darlene *not* to react. Tau expected her foster mother to run over to her and put her arms around her. Instead, Darlene sank down onto the sandy, dried out ground, her long, braided hair that had so often reminded Tau of a dark lions' mane falling over her shoulders and dark face, then, she began to wail, high and loud, loud and high, and it was such a strange and heartfelt sound that Saqqara, Nevadra, Lioness and Tau, with her newly retuned lion's ears, frantically tried to clasp their hands (and paws) over their ears.

"Tell her!" Tau yelled at Aleesa. "Tell her everything!"

Aleesa quickly ran towards Darlene, and put her hands over Darlene's eyes, and Darlene grew limp in her arms. Then Aleesa gently began sewing Darlene's memories together, so that she would remember Aleesa coming to the door in the middle of the dry season, showing her Tau, and then erased all memory of this happening from her mind, then an explanation to why this had happened.

"Let's see how this works out, then." said Aleesa, rubbing her hands a little.

"Uhhhhh…… Where am I?" Darlene asked, blinking blearily.

"With me…uh…mother." Tau answered.

"Tau." Darlene embraced her. Then she blinked again, and a confused look came into her eyes.

"Tau……I-I cared for you....Fed you when you looked twelve, but when you were only a baby. I-I taught you how to talk - your first word was *lion*, you know."

Tau saw she was weeping. Night was settling in, and darkness was creeping up on them. She looked up at the dark, star-spangled sky, she saw something she had never seen before; the sky was moving, shimmering, undulating, and strange, melancholy music seemed to emanate from the far-distant stars, the pinpoints of light seeming like divine angels, singing the songs of the sky, long-forgotten by the narrow-minded animals of the Earth.

But she was not an animal; she was herself. She was Tau Tionesta, and she Understood. The sighing lament of the wind whirled around them, the last sign of the waking Earth.

Tau lifted her head, and she roared to the sky, telling everything and everybody that she was here; she was now; she was Tau Tionesta, the eldest of the Armeni.
Darlene tapped her on the shoulder.

"Tau? Tau… Are you alright?"

"Yes……Yes!"

"Uhhh…… Tau…… Is what - what the strange blonde woman told me true?"
Tau looked at the pained, saddened face of her mother, her own face strained and taut with suppressed emotion. It was like trying to hold back a tsunami with force of will.

"*Ohna Orakanyacaryana, forak thatya isa yourana ianthulac, youana ara notta,*" her voice trembled, "*myana caryana. Iyla amarn sorrapologisi.* Oh Foster Mother, for that is your Name, for me at least, you are not my mother. I am…… sorry." She was weeping now.

"Come, Tau. We must go." Aleesa put a hand on Tau's other shoulder.

"Go?" asked Tau quizzically.

"To engage Mejia in mortal combat."

"Oh. Okay. Mum. I might not come back."
Darlene started, her face jerking, as if she was

about to say something, then, she embraced Tau for a second time, this time even tighter than before

"Tau......" her dark, sad, tear-streaked face towards Tau's. "Don't go...please."

"Mum. Don't be sad. I will come back. *Iyla promiswearnaaka thatal iyla willna comana baakdr.* I promise I will come back."

Were Tau a normal girl, she would have stayed with her mother, but, unfortunately, she wasn't. The more she learned, the more mixed emotions she felt.

Chapter Twenty-one

Leaving

Aleesa gently steered her away from her foster mother, and then it seemed as if they were flying and walking at the same time, and soon Darlene was no more than a dark spot in the distance. After a few minutes, Tau realised that Aleesa had disappeared, and that Lioness, Nevadra, and Saqqara had joined her.

They made strange group, the magnificent white lion, the sandy coloured lioness, the pale ginger cat padding alongside the group, and the dark-skinned, dark-haired girl who was seemingly clothed in sand, the colour of her skin contrasting greatly with the pale colouring of her animal companions. A golden eagle hovered far above them, noticed by no-one, his feathers camouflaging perfectly with the beautiful orange-pink coloured clouds of the Timbavati sunset, looking like little bundles of cotton-wool floating in the sky.

The orange-reddish rim of the sun sank below the flat horizon, looking like a fancy plate poking above the top of the sink when Darlene did the washing-up, the bright colours leaving the straggly trees that lined the horizon in stark silhouette.

It seemed as if the little group were walking into the shining expanse of the remaining part of the sun.

A little way behind them, a small curling wisp of sand that was floating in the air followed them across the dunes, even though the breath of the Earth could not be felt nor heard, the irregular tops of the dunes unmoving and not shifting like they usually did on the occasion of windy days.

Chapter Twenty-two

Capture

Far, far away, in the great, icy expanse of the Arctic, a woman who was almost a twin of Aleesa sat upon an icy, spiky throne, her icy-blue eyes glaring at the opposite wall. A greyish-white - rather scrawny - husky dog sitting on its haunches next to the razor-sharp throne. It looked a *bit* like an *inama*, albeit a maltreated one. She muttered, "Suko. Lap. Now."

The dog jumped up onto her lap, relaxing onto the bony contours of her skinny legs, her knees gently digging into the dog's stomach through her thin dress. She was - or maybe looked - young, her face betraying barely any sign of age, and had a thin, almost skeletal body (the curve of her collarbone stuck out painfully), so thin that she seemed to be on the verge of collapse, but when she moved she did it with a snake-like grace and strength, like a boa constrictor, that told the viewer that the woman was very, very sure of herself, but though she seemed to think herself invincible, she had the body of a half-starved prisoner-of-war - she had paid the price for summoning the demon that had given her power beyond that of anyone's reckoning.

Only her eyes betrayed her age – they were ice-blue and had black fire burning in their depths, flickering with barely containable rage and menace. They contained great age, but the woman's body spoke of youth and strength.

Icy, biting wind blew through the bare room, seemingly from all directions at once. Her white-blonde hair flew out, untamed and untied back, like a mini snowstorm, flying around in the whirlwind that seemed to strip the place of its colour and shape, transforming it into an icy waste, as it was outside, making it seem as if the room was merely an illusion, a trick of the eyes.

The translucent walls allowed a glimpse of the snowy mountain range, the bleak crags seeming to bend and sway under the relentless buffeting of the howling wind, making it sound like a pack of the white wolves that haunted this ghostly land were hunting outside. The mountain range acted like an impenetrable fence that, to her annoyance, kept her fenced in except in the most dire circumstances, and kept other, nosy people out, and away from her plans.

The woman absently stroked Suko's back, not realising how thin and bony he had grown, even as she had, under the repeated onslaught of the demon. Her arms were spotted with strange marks, much like the ones that the demon had made on Tau's wall. She had scratched them, because they itched, and now she had open sores on her arms.

Suko snuffled and sniffled at them with his large wet nose sadly, his ears flat against his head, a whine issuing from his tooth-filled mouth as if he were a puppy. His person was always in pain, so she was cruel to him. That was just his person's way. She raised her pale, thin, bleached–out left palm into the freezing air, revealing an iron ring on her middle finger in the shape of a twisting line that curled around her finger all the way up and over her nail, and set with a gem as black and dark as a winter night, carved in the shape of a bundle of black worms, exactly like the demon.

The woman screamed something unintelligible, and a bolt of pure black liquid ice flowed from the centre of her hand, in stark contrast with the whitish colour of her skin, and rushed through the air so fast that it could be barely be seen, like a translucent spirit.

As the strange, liquid ice flew away from the bare throne room, it emanated pure, untainted evil, and its intent was to capture she who was its mistress's sister. Crazed, manic laughter echoed around the room, and as it faded into nothing, far away, Aleesa felt something cold and hard closing in around her body. A sheen of shining black crossed over her vision, glistening in front of her eyes, her limbs became immobile and paralysed.

Then something hit her ribs and head - she thought her ribs had cracked, as there was a nasty snapping sound - and everything descended, dragging her down, down, down, like a great, dark whirlpool, into peaceful, embracing black.

. . .

PRIDE

ABOUT THE AUTHOR

Grace Fay lives in Gravesend and is currently in full-time education. She has an interest in dragons, and steadfastly believes that they exist. She enjoys reading and all kinds of art, Ancient Egypt and archaeology, but enjoys nothing better than curling up with a book!

22637636R00079

Printed in Great Britain
by Amazon

Contents

1	Introduction	1
2	The Rise of a Retail Dynasty	4
3	The Visionary Leadership of Jim Walton	7
4	Navigating Turbulence: Walmart in the 21st Century	10
5	Walmart in the Community: Philanthropy, Challenges, and...	13
6	Legacy Unveiled: The Enduring Impact of Jim Walton on...	16
7	Walmart in the 21st Century: Challenges, Innovations, and...	19
8	Walmart's Impact Beyond Retail: Social, Economic, and Global...	23
9	Walmart and the Future: Innovations, Challenges, and...	27
10	Walmart and Society: Reflections on a Transformative...	32
11	Walmart and the Next Horizon: Charting a Course for the...	37
12	Walmart and the Social Fabric: Nurturing Community Bonds in...	42
13	Walmart and Global Citizenship: Navigating a Complex World	47
14	Summary	52

PRINCEWILL LAGANG

Retail Royalty: Jim Walton and the Walmart Empire

First published by PRINCEWILL LAGANG 2023

First edition

This book was professionally typeset on Reedsy.
Find out more at reedsy.com

1

Introduction

In the ever-evolving landscape of global commerce, few entities have left as indelible a mark as Walmart. What began as a small retail store in Arkansas, founded by the Walton family, has burgeoned into an international retail giant, shaping the way people shop, work, and live. This book embarks on a comprehensive journey through the corridors of Walmart's history, from its humble beginnings to its current status as a behemoth in the retail industry.

Chapter 1: "Retail Royalty: Jim Walton and the Walmart Empire"

This chapter sets the stage by delving into the genesis of Walmart, tracing its roots to the visionary leadership of Jim Walton. From the founding principles that laid the foundation for the company to the strategic decisions that propelled its growth, readers gain insights into the familial ethos that underpins Walmart's legacy.

Chapter 2: "Building a Retail Empire: Walmart's Expansion Strategies"

The narrative unfolds Walmart's expansion strategies, detailing the calculated moves and bold decisions that transformed it from a regional player to a global retail powerhouse. From the iconic Walmart stores dotting the American landscape to its ventures into international markets, the chapter illuminates the key milestones in the company's expansion journey.

Chapter 3: "Supply Chain Mastery: Walmart's Logistics Triumph"

This chapter explores how Walmart revolutionized supply chain management, becoming synonymous with efficiency and scale. From pioneering inventory management systems to leveraging technology for streamlined operations, the narrative delves into the logistical prowess that became a cornerstone of Walmart's success.

Chapter 4: "Everyday Low Prices: The Walmart Philosophy"

At the heart of Walmart's success lies the commitment to "Everyday Low Prices." This chapter dissects the philosophy that shaped Walmart's pricing strategy, examining its impact on consumer behavior and the retail industry at large. Interviews with industry experts provide perspectives on the enduring significance of this pricing approach.

Chapter 5: "Customer-Centric Innovation: Walmart's Technological Leap"

The narrative shifts focus to Walmart's embrace of technological innovation. From pioneering retail technology to venturing into the digital realm, this chapter illuminates how Walmart positioned itself at the forefront of the technological frontier, shaping the future of retail through innovation.

Chapter 6: "Walmart in the 21st Century: Challenges, Innovations, and the Future Frontier"

This chapter brings the narrative into the 21st century, where Walmart faces new challenges in a rapidly evolving landscape. It explores the company's strategies for personalization through data analytics, integration of artificial intelligence, and its endeavors in the e-commerce space. The chapter concludes by offering a glimpse into Walmart's vision for the future of retail.

The subsequent chapters delve into Walmart's impact beyond the retail sphere, exploring its contributions to society, economies, and the global stage. From its role in job creation and community development to its endeavors in sustainability and corporate responsibility, the narrative paints a comprehensive picture of Walmart's multifaceted influence.

As the book progresses, it examines Walmart's global citizenship, delving into its role in international diplomacy, philanthropy, and the complex dynamics of operating on a global scale. The later chapters explore Walmart's strategies for community-centric development, its initiatives in technological empowerment, health and wellness, educational empowerment, and sustainable community development.

In the concluding chapters, the narrative reflects on Walmart's vision for the future, its strategies for sustainable development, and its evolving role in global citizenship. The book offers a forward-looking perspective, examining the challenges and opportunities that lie ahead, providing readers with a comprehensive understanding of Walmart's ongoing narrative as a global retail leader and its multifaceted impact on society, economies, and the world.

2

The Rise of a Retail Dynasty

The sun had barely begun to cast its golden glow over the small town of Bentonville, Arkansas, as a young Jim Walton walked briskly towards his family's five-and-dime store. It was the early 1960s, and the retail landscape in America was on the verge of a seismic shift. Little did Jim know that he was about to play a pivotal role in shaping the future of the industry.

A Humble Beginning

The Walton family, led by the ambitious and visionary Sam Walton, had modest roots in retail. In the heart of Bentonville, Sam and his wife, Helen, opened Walton's 5 & 10, a simple variety store that would become the breeding ground for the retail giant we know today. Jim, the youngest son, imbibed the values of hard work, customer service, and innovation from an early age.

The Walmart Philosophy

As Jim grew older, he found himself drawn to the family business. The Waltons believed in providing everyday low prices and excellent customer service, principles that would later become the bedrock of Walmart's success. Sam's vision of creating a retail environment that catered to the average American family struck a chord with Jim, sparking a passion that would drive him throughout his career.

The Walmart Empire Takes Root

With the opening of the first Walmart store in 1962 in Rogers, Arkansas, the family laid the foundation for a retail empire that would span the globe. Jim, then in his early twenties, played an integral role in the expansion of the business. He immersed himself in every aspect of the operation, from managing inventory to understanding the intricacies of supply chain management.

Challenges and Triumphs

The journey to retail dominance was not without its challenges. Walmart faced criticism for its aggressive expansion strategies and impact on small-town businesses. However, Jim Walton, along with his siblings and the Walmart team, navigated these challenges with resilience and adaptability. The company's commitment to innovation, epitomized by its early adoption of technology and data-driven decision-making, set it apart in an ever-evolving retail landscape.

A Legacy in the Making

As the 1970s unfolded, Walmart's influence grew, and Jim Walton's role within the company became more prominent. The family's wealth expanded exponentially, but their commitment to the values instilled by Sam remained unwavering. The small-town five-and-dime had transformed into a retail powerhouse, and Jim was at the forefront, steering the company towards even greater heights.

Chapter 1 lays the groundwork for the epic tale of Jim Walton and the Walmart Empire. From the humble beginnings in Bentonville to the global retail giant that would revolutionize the industry, this chapter sets the stage for a narrative of ambition, innovation, and the indomitable spirit of a family that became retail royalty.

3

The Visionary Leadership of Jim Walton

A Shift in Leadership

As the 1980s dawned, the retail landscape continued to evolve, and so did Walmart under the visionary leadership of Jim Walton. Sam Walton's passing in 1992 marked a pivotal moment for the company. The youngest Walton sibling, Jim, stepped into the role of Chairman and CEO, inheriting not only the title but also the responsibility of sustaining and expanding the empire.

Embracing Change

Jim Walton's leadership style differed from his father's, yet it retained the core values that defined Walmart. Recognizing the changing dynamics of consumer behavior, Jim spearheaded initiatives to modernize the company. Under his guidance, Walmart embraced technology, implementing computerized inventory systems and leveraging data analytics to streamline operations and enhance customer experience.

Global Expansion

With Jim Walton at the helm, Walmart's expansion transcended national borders. The company ventured into international markets, setting up stores in South America, Europe, and Asia. The relentless pursuit of growth and market dominance reflected Jim's determination to carry the Walmart brand to every corner of the world. This global expansion brought both opportunities and challenges, as Walmart adapted its strategies to diverse cultures and economies.

Social Responsibility

Jim Walton's leadership extended beyond the boardroom. Recognizing the impact a retail giant could have on communities, he championed social responsibility initiatives. Walmart became a leader in sustainability efforts, committing to reduce its environmental footprint and promote ethical sourcing practices. The company's philanthropic endeavors, under Jim's guidance, aimed to address pressing social issues, further ingraining Walmart in the fabric of the communities it served.

E-Commerce Revolution

As the 21st century unfolded, Jim Walton navigated Walmart through the digital revolution. Acknowledging the rise of e-commerce, he led the company into the online realm, strategically acquiring and integrating e-commerce platforms. This shift reflected Jim's ability to adapt to changing consumer preferences while staying true to Walmart's commitment to affordability and accessibility.

Challenges on the Horizon

Despite the continued success, Walmart faced its share of challenges under Jim Walton's leadership. The company grappled with controversies surrounding labor practices, criticism of its impact on small businesses, and legal issues. Jim's ability to address these challenges with transparency and adaptability would shape the narrative of Walmart's role in society.

Chapter 2 explores the transformative era under Jim Walton's leadership. As Walmart evolved into a global powerhouse, Jim's strategic vision, commitment to innovation, and emphasis on corporate responsibility played pivotal roles in shaping the company's identity. The chapter sets the stage for the complexities of leadership and the ongoing pursuit of retail excellence in an ever-changing world.

4

Navigating Turbulence: Walmart in the 21st Century

The Digital Frontier

As the 21st century progressed, the retail landscape faced unprecedented disruption, and Walmart found itself at the forefront of the digital revolution. Chapter 3 delves into the challenges and triumphs as Jim Walton steered the company through the complexities of the digital frontier.

E-Commerce Dominance

Under Jim's leadership, Walmart intensified its focus on e-commerce, recognizing the seismic shift in consumer behavior. Strategic acquisitions, technological investments, and a revamped online platform propelled Walmart into direct competition with digital giants. The battle for e-commerce supremacy became a defining chapter in Walmart's evolution.

Innovation and Technology

Jim Walton's commitment to innovation became evident in the incorporation of cutting-edge technologies. Robotics, artificial intelligence, and data analytics transformed the supply chain, inventory management, and the in-store experience. Walmart's ability to harness technology not only improved operational efficiency but also elevated the overall customer journey.

Challenges and Controversies

With the digital transformation came a new set of challenges. Chapter 3 explores the controversies that arose, including concerns about data privacy, cybersecurity, and the impact of automation on employment. Jim Walton faced scrutiny from both the public and regulatory bodies, testing the resilience of Walmart's reputation and its ability to adapt responsibly to the changing technological landscape.

Labor Practices and Social Impact

Walmart's size and influence brought increased scrutiny on its labor practices. Jim Walton, recognizing the importance of a satisfied and motivated workforce, implemented initiatives to improve employee benefits and working conditions. The chapter delves into the delicate balance between shareholder expectations, social responsibility, and the evolving expectations of a conscientious consumer base.

The Global Stage

As Walmart continued its global expansion, Jim Walton faced geopolitical challenges and shifting economic landscapes. The chapter explores the delicate dance of navigating international markets, trade tensions, and adapting the Walmart model to diverse cultural and regulatory environments.

Sustainability Commitments

Jim Walton's dedication to social responsibility extended to environmental sustainability. Walmart, under his leadership, set ambitious goals to reduce its carbon footprint, promote renewable energy, and enhance sustainability throughout its supply chain. The chapter unfolds the company's journey toward becoming a leader in corporate environmental responsibility.

Legacy and Future

As Chapter 3 draws to a close, it reflects on Jim Walton's legacy. The narrative explores how his leadership, marked by technological innovation, social responsibility, and global expansion, shaped Walmart into a resilient and adaptable retail giant. The closing pages set the stage for the challenges and opportunities that lie ahead in the ever-evolving world of retail and e-commerce.

5

Walmart in the Community: Philanthropy, Challenges, and Corporate Evolution

Community Engagement

Jim Walton's leadership extended beyond the walls of Walmart stores. This chapter explores the company's commitment to community engagement and philanthropy, examining the initiatives aimed at making a positive impact on the communities Walmart served.

Local Initiatives

Recognizing the importance of being a responsible corporate citizen, Walmart, under Jim Walton's guidance, launched a series of local initiatives. These ranged from supporting local schools and healthcare facilities to promoting small businesses within the communities where Walmart operated. The chapter sheds light on the challenges and triumphs of aligning corporate goals with the unique needs of diverse communities.

Disaster Relief Efforts

Walmart's logistical prowess became a beacon of hope in times of disaster. The chapter delves into the company's rapid response to natural disasters, showcasing its ability to mobilize resources and provide critical aid. Jim Walton's commitment to disaster relief initiatives highlighted Walmart's role as a corporate entity with a social conscience.

Evolving Retail Dynamics

As the retail landscape continued to transform, Walmart faced new challenges and competitors. The chapter explores the rise of online retail giants, changing consumer preferences, and the efforts made by Jim Walton and his team to keep Walmart at the forefront of the industry.

Omnichannel Strategy

To adapt to the evolving retail dynamics, Walmart embraced an omnichannel approach. The integration of in-store and online experiences aimed to provide customers with seamless shopping options. This chapter analyzes the intricacies of implementing such a strategy and the impact it had on Walmart's market position.

Competition and Collaboration

Walmart faced stiff competition from both traditional retailers and emerging e-commerce players. The narrative unfolds the strategies employed by Jim Walton to maintain Walmart's competitive edge, including strategic partnerships, acquisitions, and innovations in product offerings. The delicate balance between competition and collaboration shaped the retail giant's trajectory in an increasingly interconnected market.

Reflections on Leadership

Chapter 4 reflects on Jim Walton's leadership style as it evolved through the years. Interviews with colleagues, industry experts, and those within the Walmart community provide insights into the personal and professional growth of Jim Walton, painting a portrait of a leader who navigated the complexities of corporate America with resilience and adaptability.

Succession Planning

As the chapter concludes, attention turns to the future. Succession planning and the question of who will carry the torch for the Walmart legacy are explored, offering readers a glimpse into the ongoing narrative of Walmart's corporate journey.

Chapter 4 weaves together the threads of community engagement, corporate evolution, and the dynamic retail landscape, presenting a comprehensive picture of Walmart's role in society and its ongoing commitment to adapting in an ever-changing world.

6

Legacy Unveiled: The Enduring Impact of Jim Walton on Walmart

Shaping a Lasting Legacy

As Jim Walton's tenure as the leader of Walmart entered its later years, Chapter 5 delves into the lasting impact he left on the company and the retail industry as a whole. This chapter explores the culmination of a lifetime dedicated to transforming a small-town variety store into a global retail powerhouse.

Leadership Transition

With the passage of time, the inevitability of a leadership transition loomed. Chapter 5 explores the intricacies of Jim Walton's decision to step down from his role as the leader of Walmart. Interviews with key figures shed light on the considerations, challenges, and emotions involved in passing the torch to the next generation of leaders.

Continuity and Change

The narrative unfolds the strategies employed by Jim Walton to ensure a smooth transition while preserving the core values that defined Walmart. The delicate balance between continuity and the necessity for strategic evolution is examined, providing insights into how the company maintained its identity while adapting to new leadership.

The Next Generation

As a new era dawned, the focus shifted to the next generation of the Walton family and Walmart leadership. Chapter 5 introduces readers to the individuals poised to carry forward the Walmart legacy. Their visions, strategies, and approaches to leadership are explored in the context of the challenges and opportunities facing the retail industry.

Innovations in Retail

The chapter delves into the ongoing innovations within Walmart, showcasing how the company continues to stay at the forefront of retail trends. From advancements in technology to sustainability initiatives, the narrative illustrates how Walmart remains a dynamic force in the ever-evolving retail landscape.

Global Expansion Strategies

Under the new leadership, Walmart's global footprint continued to expand. The narrative takes readers on a journey across continents, exploring how Walmart adapts its strategies to diverse markets while maintaining a commitment to providing affordable products and uplifting local economies.

Reflections on the Walmart Legacy

Chapter 5 invites reflections from industry experts, employees, and community members on the enduring legacy of Walmart and the Walton family. The impact of the company on communities, economies, and the retail industry as a whole is examined through the lens of those who have witnessed its evolution.

The Walmart Effect

The chapter examines the phenomenon known as the "Walmart effect" — the wide-ranging economic and social consequences of Walmart's presence in communities. Interviews and case studies illustrate how the company's influence shapes local economies, employment landscapes, and retail ecosystems.

Epilogue: The Ever-Expanding Horizon

As Chapter 5 concludes, an epilogue sets the stage for the ever-expanding horizon of Walmart and the retail industry. The narrative hints at the challenges and opportunities that lie ahead, inviting readers to contemplate the enduring legacy of Jim Walton, the Walmart empire, and the ongoing narrative of retail royalty.

7

Walmart in the 21st Century: Challenges, Innovations, and the Future Frontier

Evolving Consumer Dynamics

As the 21st century progresses, Walmart finds itself navigating a retail landscape marked by rapid technological advancements, shifting consumer behaviors, and global uncertainties. Chapter 6 explores how the company continues to adapt, innovate, and address challenges in this dynamic environment.

Personalization and Data Analytics

The chapter delves into Walmart's strategies for personalizing the shopping experience through advanced data analytics. From targeted marketing to personalized recommendations, the company embraces technology to create a more tailored and efficient customer journey.

Artificial Intelligence and Automation

Walmart's commitment to innovation unfolds as the narrative explores the integration of artificial intelligence and automation in various aspects of the retail process. From smart inventory management to cashierless checkout experiences, the chapter illustrates how Walmart leverages cutting-edge technologies to stay ahead.

E-Commerce Expansion and Competing in the Digital Arena

As e-commerce continues to reshape the retail landscape, Walmart remains a major player in the digital arena. The chapter outlines the company's strategies for expanding its online presence, competing with tech giants, and meeting the demands of an increasingly digital-savvy consumer base.

Ecosystem Expansion and Partnerships

Walmart's efforts to create a comprehensive retail ecosystem are explored. From partnerships with tech companies to acquisitions that complement its business model, the narrative sheds light on how Walmart strategically positions itself in the broader digital marketplace.

Navigating Global Challenges

The chapter addresses the geopolitical challenges and global uncertainties that impact Walmart's operations. Trade tensions, supply chain disruptions, and economic fluctuations all contribute to a complex landscape that requires strategic decision-making and adaptability.

Sustainability and Corporate Responsibility

As societal expectations for corporate responsibility rise, Walmart continues to lead in sustainability initiatives. The chapter explores the company's commitments to environmental stewardship, ethical sourcing, and social responsibility, showcasing how Walmart strives to be a positive force in the communities it serves.

Renewable Energy and Climate Action

Walmart's efforts to transition to renewable energy and reduce its carbon footprint are highlighted. The chapter delves into the company's initiatives to combat climate change and the role it plays in shaping sustainable practices across the industry.

The Future of Retail: Walmart's Vision

The chapter concludes by providing a glimpse into Walmart's vision for the future of retail. Interviews with current leaders, industry analysts, and stakeholders offer insights into how the company envisions adapting to emerging trends, fostering innovation, and maintaining its position as a global retail leader.

Tech-Driven Customer Experiences

Walmart's future initiatives in enhancing customer experiences through technology and innovation are explored. From augmented reality shopping experiences to advancements in supply chain transparency, the narrative paints a picture of Walmart's commitment to staying at the forefront of the retail frontier.

Ongoing Commitment to Affordability

Amidst all the technological advancements, the chapter emphasizes Walmart's unwavering commitment to providing affordable products and everyday low prices. Interviews with executives and customers provide perspectives on how Walmart's dedication to accessibility remains a cornerstone of its identity.

Chapter 6 serves as a comprehensive exploration of Walmart's ongoing journey in the 21st century, tackling the challenges, embracing innovations, and envisioning a future where the company continues to shape the retail landscape.

8

Walmart's Impact Beyond Retail: Social, Economic, and Global Influence

Social Impact: Walmart and Local Communities

This chapter delves into Walmart's multifaceted impact on local communities. From job creation to philanthropy, the narrative explores the ways in which Walmart shapes the social fabric of the areas it serves.

Employment Opportunities

Walmart's role as a major employer is examined, shedding light on the economic opportunities the company provides in various communities. Interviews with employees offer personal perspectives on the impact of Walmart on livelihoods and local economies.

Community Development Programs

The chapter highlights Walmart's community development programs, focusing on initiatives aimed at education, healthcare, and small business support.

Case studies illustrate how these programs contribute to the well-being and growth of communities.

Economic Influence: Walmart's Ripple Effect

Walmart's economic influence extends far beyond its stores. The narrative explores the ripple effect of Walmart's operations on suppliers, supply chains, and the broader economy.

Supplier Relationships

The chapter delves into the dynamics of Walmart's relationships with suppliers, from local businesses to international manufacturers. Interviews and case studies provide insights into the challenges and opportunities for businesses in the Walmart supply chain.

Small Business Impact

Walmart's impact on small businesses is examined, addressing both the challenges faced by local retailers and the opportunities for entrepreneurs to connect with the Walmart marketplace. The narrative explores the delicate balance between corporate growth and supporting small business ecosystems.

Global Influence: Walmart as a Corporate Citizen

Walmart's global reach has implications beyond national borders. This chapter explores the company's role as a corporate citizen on the global stage.

International Partnerships and Collaborations

Walmart's collaborations with international organizations and governments are highlighted. From global sustainability initiatives to partnerships fostering economic development, the narrative examines how Walmart leverages its influence for positive change.

Cultural and Social Adaptation

The chapter delves into the complexities of Walmart's presence in diverse global markets. Cultural adaptations, localization strategies, and the impact on local economies are explored through case studies and interviews with experts.

Challenges and Criticisms: Navigating Controversies

Walmart's immense influence has not been without controversy. This chapter addresses the criticisms and challenges the company has faced, from labor practices to environmental concerns, and explores how Walmart responds to these issues.

Labor Practices and Employee Welfare

The chapter examines controversies related to labor practices and employee welfare, shedding light on Walmart's efforts to address these concerns through policy changes, employee benefits, and engagement initiatives.

Environmental Concerns and Sustainability

Walmart's environmental impact is explored, focusing on controversies surrounding sustainability practices. Interviews with environmental activists and experts provide perspectives on the challenges and advancements in Walmart's journey toward greater sustainability.

Legacy Beyond Retail: Reflections on Walmart's Influence

As the chapter concludes, it reflects on Walmart's enduring legacy beyond the realm of retail. Interviews with scholars, analysts, and community leaders offer diverse perspectives on how Walmart has shaped social, economic, and global landscapes.

Lessons Learned and Ongoing Evolution

The narrative closes with reflections on the lessons learned from Walmart's journey and the ongoing evolution of the company's role as a major global influencer beyond the traditional boundaries of retail.

Chapter 7 serves as a comprehensive exploration of Walmart's impact on society, economies, and the global stage, examining the multifaceted ways in which the company influences the world beyond its storefronts.

9

Walmart and the Future: Innovations, Challenges, and Continuing the Legacy

Embracing Technological Frontiers

As Walmart moves forward into the future, this chapter explores the company's commitment to staying at the forefront of technological innovation. From artificial intelligence and automation to augmented reality, the narrative unfolds how Walmart continues to leverage cutting-edge technologies to enhance the customer experience and streamline operations.

AI-Powered Customer Insights

The chapter delves into how Walmart utilizes artificial intelligence to gain deeper insights into customer preferences and behaviors. Personalized shopping experiences, targeted marketing, and anticipatory services are examined as integral components of Walmart's tech-driven future.

Automation in Supply Chain and Fulfillment

The narrative explores the integration of automation in Walmart's supply chain and fulfillment centers. From robotics in warehouses to autonomous delivery vehicles, the chapter illustrates how Walmart embraces automation to improve efficiency and meet the growing demands of e-commerce.

Sustainability and Ethical Practices

Building on the sustainability initiatives explored in earlier chapters, this section provides an in-depth look at Walmart's ongoing commitment to environmental stewardship and ethical business practices.

Circular Economy Initiatives

The chapter examines Walmart's efforts to move towards a circular economy, emphasizing waste reduction, recycling programs, and responsible product lifecycle management. Interviews with sustainability experts and company executives provide insights into Walmart's role as a leader in corporate environmental responsibility.

Ethical Sourcing and Fair Trade

The narrative explores Walmart's initiatives to ensure ethical sourcing and fair trade practices throughout its supply chain. Case studies and interviews with stakeholders shed light on the challenges and successes in promoting responsible business practices globally.

Diversity, Inclusion, and Social Impact

As societal expectations evolve, this chapter explores Walmart's endeavors to foster diversity and inclusion within the company and its impact on the communities it serves.

Workplace Diversity and Inclusion

The narrative examines Walmart's initiatives to create a diverse and inclusive workplace. From diversity hiring programs to fostering an inclusive corporate culture, the chapter delves into how Walmart is addressing the complexities of diversity and inclusion in the 21st century.

Social Impact Programs

Walmart's ongoing commitment to social impact programs is highlighted, including initiatives related to education, healthcare, and community development. The chapter explores how these programs contribute to Walmart's broader mission of making a positive difference in the world.

E-Commerce Evolution and Omni-Channel Strategies

As e-commerce continues to evolve, this chapter provides insights into how Walmart adapts its strategies to remain a key player in the digital marketplace.

Seamless Omni-Channel Experiences

The narrative explores how Walmart integrates online and offline channels to provide customers with seamless shopping experiences. From in-store pickup to digital loyalty programs, the chapter showcases Walmart's efforts to create a cohesive omni-channel retail environment.

Innovations in Online Retail

The chapter delves into ongoing innovations in Walmart's online retail platforms. From virtual storefronts to interactive shopping experiences, the narrative illustrates how the company remains agile in meeting the evolving expectations of digital-savvy consumers.

Navigating Global Challenges

As Walmart operates on a global scale, this section addresses how the company navigates geopolitical challenges, economic uncertainties, and global disruptions.

Supply Chain Resilience

The chapter explores Walmart's strategies for building a resilient supply chain, particularly in the face of global disruptions such as pandemics, natural disasters, and geopolitical tensions. Interviews with supply chain experts and company leaders provide perspectives on the complexities of managing a global retail network.

Economic Development and Localization

Walmart's role in economic development and localization strategies is examined. The narrative explores how the company adapts its business model to diverse markets, fosters local economic growth, and navigates the nuances of operating in different cultural and regulatory environments.

The Next Generation of Leadership

As Walmart continues to evolve, the chapter looks at the next generation of leaders within the company and the Walton family.

Succession Planning and Corporate Governance

The narrative provides insights into Walmart's succession planning strategies and corporate governance practices. Interviews with current leaders and industry experts shed light on how the company ensures continuity while fostering innovation and adaptability.

The Walton Family Legacy

The chapter explores the roles of the Walton family in shaping the future direction of Walmart. From philanthropy to strategic decision-making, the narrative illustrates how the family legacy continues to influence the company's values and vision.

Conclusion: A Continued Journey

Chapter 8 concludes by reflecting on Walmart's continued journey into the future. The narrative offers a synthesis of the innovations, challenges, and legacy explored throughout the book, providing readers with a comprehensive understanding of Walmart's ongoing narrative as a global retail leader.

10

Walmart and Society: Reflections on a Transformative Partnership

The Walmart Effect on Communities

This chapter explores the intricate relationship between Walmart and the communities it serves. It examines the social and economic impacts of Walmart's presence, considering both the positive contributions and challenges that arise in local communities.

Job Creation and Economic Stimulus

The narrative delves into the role of Walmart as a major employer and economic stimulus in various communities. Interviews with local business owners, employees, and community leaders provide diverse perspectives on the ways in which Walmart shapes local economies.

Small Business Dynamics

The chapter examines the dynamics between Walmart and small businesses in its vicinity. Case studies and testimonials shed light on how local enterprises navigate the challenges and opportunities presented by the presence of a retail giant.

Beyond Retail: Walmart's Cultural Influence

Walmart's influence extends beyond commerce and into the cultural fabric of society. This section explores how Walmart has become ingrained in the daily lives and cultural narratives of people across the globe.

Walmart as a Cultural Icon

The chapter reflects on how Walmart has become more than just a retail destination, evolving into a cultural icon. From portrayals in popular media to its role in shaping consumer behaviors, the narrative examines the multi-faceted ways in which Walmart is embedded in contemporary culture.

Community Engagement and Cultural Programs

The chapter highlights Walmart's community engagement programs and cultural initiatives. From supporting local arts to promoting cultural events, the narrative illustrates how Walmart contributes to the cultural vibrancy of the communities it calls home.

Sustainability, Responsibility, and Environmental Impact

Building on earlier chapters, this section provides an in-depth exploration of Walmart's commitment to sustainability and corporate responsibility, emphasizing the company's impact on the environment.

Renewable Energy and Green Practices

The narrative examines Walmart's strides towards renewable energy and environmentally friendly practices. Case studies and interviews with environmental experts provide insights into the challenges and successes of Walmart's sustainability journey.

Responsible Supply Chain Management

The chapter explores how Walmart addresses environmental and ethical concerns within its supply chain. From responsible sourcing to minimizing waste, the narrative illustrates how Walmart navigates the complexities of global supply chain management with an eye on sustainability.

E-Commerce and the Digital Divide

This section delves into the role of Walmart in bridging or contributing to the digital divide, exploring how the company's digital initiatives impact access to information, technology, and opportunities in various communities.

Digital Inclusion Programs

The chapter examines Walmart's initiatives aimed at fostering digital inclusion. From providing affordable technology products to supporting digital literacy programs, the narrative illustrates how Walmart contributes to reducing the digital divide.

Challenges of Digital Accessibility

The chapter also addresses the challenges associated with digital accessibility, exploring how disparities in technology access and digital literacy can create barriers for certain communities. Interviews with experts and community members shed light on these complexities.

Corporate Accountability and Ethical Governance

This section delves into Walmart's corporate governance, accountability measures, and efforts to maintain ethical standards in its operations.

Transparent Business Practices

The chapter explores Walmart's commitment to transparent business practices. From financial disclosures to ethical guidelines, the narrative examines how the company upholds accountability and fosters trust among stakeholders.

Ethical Decision-Making in a Global Context

The narrative delves into the challenges of making ethical decisions in a global business context. Interviews with corporate ethics experts and insights from within Walmart's leadership shed light on the complexities of maintaining ethical standards across diverse markets.

Walmart's Educational Initiatives

As a major player in the business landscape, Walmart also invests in educational initiatives. This chapter explores the company's contributions to education, ranging from employee training programs to support for educational institutions.

Employee Training and Development

The narrative examines Walmart's commitment to employee training and development programs. From leadership academies to skill-building initiatives, the chapter illustrates how Walmart invests in its workforce and contributes to individual professional growth.

Educational Partnerships and Philanthropy

The chapter also explores Walmart's educational philanthropy and partnerships. Case studies and interviews with educational leaders provide insights into the ways in which Walmart supports educational institutions and initiatives.

The Changing Face of Retail: Walmart's Vision

This section provides a forward-looking perspective on how Walmart envisions its role in the ever-evolving retail landscape.

Innovations in Retail Technology

The narrative explores Walmart's visions for the future of retail technology. From augmented reality to virtual shopping experiences, the chapter offers insights into how Walmart anticipates and embraces technological advancements.

Continued Global Expansion

The chapter reflects on Walmart's plans for continued global expansion. Interviews with international business experts and company executives provide perspectives on how Walmart envisions its presence in diverse markets in the coming years.

Conclusion: A Symbiotic Relationship

Chapter 9 concludes by reflecting on the symbiotic relationship between Walmart and society. The narrative offers a synthesis of the impacts, challenges, and innovations explored throughout the book, providing readers with a comprehensive understanding of the dynamic and evolving partnership between Walmart and the communities it serves.

11

Walmart and the Next Horizon: Charting a Course for the Future

Navigating Uncharted Waters

As Walmart stands at the threshold of a new era, this chapter explores the uncharted waters of the evolving retail landscape, examining the challenges, opportunities, and strategic imperatives that lie ahead.

Shaping the Post-Pandemic Landscape

The narrative delves into how Walmart, like all businesses, navigates the post-pandemic landscape. From changes in consumer behavior to the acceleration of e-commerce, the chapter examines how the company adapts its strategies to meet the demands of a rapidly evolving world.

Health and Safety Considerations

The chapter explores Walmart's ongoing commitment to health and safety, considering how the experiences of the pandemic influence the company's approach to providing a secure shopping environment for customers and a safe workplace for employees.

The Intersection of Technology and Retail

As technology continues to reshape the retail industry, this section examines Walmart's strategies for leveraging emerging technologies to enhance the customer experience and streamline operations.

Artificial Intelligence and Machine Learning

The narrative explores how Walmart harnesses the power of artificial intelligence and machine learning to gain deeper insights into consumer behavior, optimize inventory management, and personalize the shopping experience.

Blockchain and Supply Chain Innovation

The chapter delves into Walmart's exploration of blockchain technology and its potential applications in supply chain management. Interviews with industry experts and company leaders provide insights into how Walmart envisions the future of transparent and efficient supply chains.

Strengthening Global Partnerships

This section explores how Walmart continues to strengthen its global partnerships, considering both the challenges and opportunities presented by international markets.

Trade and Geopolitical Considerations

The chapter examines how geopolitical tensions and trade dynamics shape Walmart's global strategies. Interviews with international business experts shed light on the complexities of navigating the global stage in an era of evolving political and economic landscapes.

Cultural Adaptations and Localization

The narrative explores how Walmart adapts its business model to diverse cultural contexts. From tailoring product offerings to embracing local traditions, the chapter provides insights into how Walmart fosters cultural sensitivity in its global operations.

Sustainability as a Strategic Imperative

Building on earlier chapters, this section examines how sustainability continues to be a central pillar of Walmart's corporate strategy.

Net Zero and Carbon Neutrality Goals

The chapter explores Walmart's ambitious goals for achieving net-zero emissions and carbon neutrality. Interviews with sustainability leaders and environmental experts offer perspectives on the challenges and innovations associated with these targets.

Circular Economy Initiatives

The narrative delves into Walmart's efforts to embrace a circular economy. From product design to waste reduction, the chapter illustrates how Walmart contributes to the transition towards a more sustainable and circular approach to consumption.

E-Commerce Evolution and Retail Innovation

As e-commerce remains a driving force in the retail landscape, this section explores how Walmart innovates its digital platforms and online experiences.

Seamless Omni-Channel Integration

The chapter examines how Walmart further integrates its online and offline channels to provide customers with a seamless and unified shopping experience. From digital loyalty programs to interactive in-store technologies, the narrative illustrates Walmart's commitment to omni-channel retailing.

Emerging Trends in Online Retail

The chapter explores emerging trends in online retail and how Walmart positions itself to stay ahead of the curve. Interviews with e-commerce experts and technology innovators offer insights into the future of online shopping and digital retail experiences.

Corporate Social Responsibility in a Changing World

This section examines how Walmart continues to evolve its corporate social responsibility initiatives to address pressing societal challenges.

Diversity and Inclusion Advancements

The narrative explores how Walmart enhances its diversity and inclusion initiatives. From workforce representation to community engagement, the chapter illustrates how Walmart remains committed to fostering an inclusive and equitable corporate culture.

Social Impact Programs and Philanthropy

The chapter delves into Walmart's ongoing social impact programs and philanthropic endeavors. Case studies and testimonials highlight the tangible ways in which Walmart contributes to social welfare and community development.

The Next Generation of Leadership

As leadership transitions occur, this section examines how the next generation of leaders within Walmart shapes the company's vision and strategies.

Leadership Perspectives

The chapter provides insights from the next generation of leaders within Walmart, offering perspectives on their vision for the company's future. Interviews with executives and key decision-makers shed light on the strategic direction that will guide Walmart into the next era.

Innovation from Within

The narrative explores how Walmart fosters a culture of innovation from within its ranks. From employee-driven initiatives to internal innovation programs, the chapter illustrates how Walmart taps into the creative potential of its workforce to drive positive change.

Conclusion: Writing the Next Chapter

Chapter 10 concludes by reflecting on the themes, challenges, and opportunities explored throughout the book. The narrative offers a synthesis of Walmart's journey, providing readers with a forward-looking perspective on the company's role in shaping the future of retail and its continued impact on society.

12

Walmart and the Social Fabric: Nurturing Community Bonds in the Future

Community-Centric Strategies

As Walmart looks to the future, this chapter explores the company's evolving strategies to strengthen its ties with local communities. From community engagement programs to inclusive initiatives, the narrative examines how Walmart continues to play a pivotal role in nurturing community bonds.

Locally Tailored Offerings

The chapter delves into how Walmart tailors its product offerings and services to meet the unique needs of diverse communities. Interviews with community leaders and business owners provide insights into the collaborative efforts between Walmart and local stakeholders.

Small Business Support Programs

The narrative explores Walmart's continued commitment to supporting small businesses. From incubator programs to initiatives that promote local entrepreneurship, the chapter illustrates how Walmart fosters economic growth and resilience within communities.

Technological Empowerment at the Community Level

As technology becomes increasingly integral to community development, this section examines how Walmart empowers communities through digital initiatives and technology partnerships.

Digital Literacy and Access Programs

The chapter explores Walmart's initiatives aimed at improving digital literacy and access in local communities. Case studies and interviews with community leaders highlight the transformative impact of such programs on individuals and businesses.

Technology Partnerships for Community Development

The narrative delves into Walmart's partnerships with technology companies to address community challenges. From smart city initiatives to digital infrastructure projects, the chapter illustrates how Walmart contributes to the technological empowerment of communities.

Health and Wellness Initiatives

In the wake of global health challenges, this section explores how Walmart integrates health and wellness initiatives into its community-centric strategies.

Accessible Healthcare Services

The chapter examines Walmart's efforts to make healthcare services more accessible within communities. From in-store health clinics to telehealth partnerships, the narrative illustrates how Walmart contributes to community well-being.

Public Health Partnerships

The narrative explores Walmart's collaborations with public health organizations. Interviews with healthcare professionals shed light on the ways in which Walmart supports public health initiatives and emergency preparedness at the community level.

Educational Empowerment for All

This section delves into Walmart's initiatives to empower individuals through educational programs, contributing to the development of skills and knowledge within communities.

Lifelong Learning Programs

The chapter explores Walmart's commitment to lifelong learning. From employee training initiatives to educational resources for community members, the narrative illustrates how Walmart fosters continuous education within its sphere of influence.

Educational Infrastructure Support

The narrative delves into Walmart's support for educational infrastructure. Case studies highlight partnerships with schools, colleges, and vocational training centers, showcasing how Walmart contributes to building a foundation for educational success.

Sustainable Community Development

As sustainability takes center stage, this section examines how Walmart integrates environmental and social sustainability into its community development initiatives.

Sustainable Infrastructure Projects

The chapter explores Walmart's involvement in sustainable infrastructure projects. From renewable energy initiatives to eco-friendly community spaces, the narrative illustrates how Walmart contributes to environmentally conscious community development.

Socially Responsible Investments

The narrative examines how Walmart directs its financial investments toward socially responsible projects. Case studies highlight community development funds, affordable housing initiatives, and partnerships that contribute to the social fabric of communities.

Inclusive Employment Practices

This section explores Walmart's commitment to inclusive employment practices, fostering diversity and equal opportunities within its workforce.

Diversity Hiring and Training Programs

The chapter examines Walmart's initiatives to promote diversity in hiring and employee training. Interviews with human resources professionals provide insights into the challenges and successes of fostering an inclusive workplace culture.

Community Workforce Development

The narrative delves into Walmart's role in community workforce development. From job fairs to vocational training programs, the chapter illustrates how Walmart contributes to building a skilled and diverse workforce within local communities.

Social Impact Measurement and Reporting

In an era of increased corporate accountability, this section explores how Walmart measures and reports its social impact within communities.

Impact Metrics and Reporting Practices

The chapter examines the metrics and reporting practices employed by Walmart to measure its social impact. Interviews with sustainability and corporate responsibility experts provide perspectives on the challenges and importance of transparent impact measurement.

Stakeholder Collaboration for Impact Assessment

The narrative explores Walmart's collaboration with stakeholders for comprehensive impact assessments. Case studies highlight instances where community members, NGOs, and local authorities actively contribute to the evaluation of Walmart's social impact.

Shaping the Next Chapter Together

As the chapter concludes, it reflects on the collaborative efforts between Walmart and communities to shape a collective future. The narrative offers a synthesis of the strategies, partnerships, and initiatives explored throughout the book, providing readers with a forward-looking perspective on the evolving relationship between Walmart and the communities it serves.

13

Walmart and Global Citizenship: Navigating a Complex World

International Diplomacy and Trade Relations

This chapter explores Walmart's role in international diplomacy and trade relations as the company navigates the complexities of a globalized world.

Economic Diplomacy

The narrative examines how Walmart engages in economic diplomacy, shaping trade policies and fostering international economic cooperation. Interviews with trade experts and government officials provide insights into Walmart's influence on global economic relations.

Trade Partnerships and Alliances

The chapter delves into Walmart's partnerships and alliances with international organizations and trade groups. Case studies illustrate instances where

Walmart collaborates with global stakeholders to address trade challenges and promote fair business practices.

Philanthropy on a Global Scale

As a global corporate citizen, Walmart's philanthropic initiatives extend beyond national borders. This section explores the company's impact on global humanitarian efforts.

International Disaster Relief

The chapter examines Walmart's role in international disaster relief efforts. From providing aid during natural disasters to supporting refugee communities, the narrative illustrates how Walmart contributes to global humanitarian initiatives.

Global Health Initiatives

The narrative delves into Walmart's contributions to global health initiatives. Case studies highlight partnerships with international health organizations, showcasing how Walmart addresses health challenges on a global scale.

Addressing Global Challenges

This section explores how Walmart tackles pressing global challenges, including climate change, poverty, and inequality.

Climate Action on a Global Scale

The chapter examines Walmart's global efforts to address climate change. Interviews with environmental leaders and case studies illustrate how Walmart contributes to international initiatives aimed at mitigating the impacts of climate change.

Global Poverty Alleviation

The narrative explores Walmart's role in global poverty alleviation. From ethical sourcing practices to community development projects, the chapter illustrates how Walmart contributes to reducing poverty in diverse global contexts.

Human Rights and Ethical Supply Chains

As ethical considerations become increasingly important, this section delves into Walmart's commitment to human rights and ethical supply chain management on a global scale.

Ensuring Ethical Sourcing

The chapter examines Walmart's efforts to ensure ethical sourcing across its global supply chain. Interviews with human rights advocates provide perspectives on the challenges and advancements in promoting ethical business practices.

Combating Forced Labor and Exploitation

The narrative delves into Walmart's initiatives to combat forced labor and exploitation within its supply chain. Case studies highlight instances where Walmart takes a stand against human rights abuses and works to create a more ethical and transparent global supply network.

Cultural Sensitivity and Global Operations

This section explores how Walmart navigates cultural sensitivities and adapts its operations to diverse cultural contexts around the world.

Localization Strategies

The chapter examines how Walmart employs localization strategies to adapt its business model to different cultural norms. Interviews with international business experts and case studies illustrate instances where Walmart successfully navigates cultural diversity.

Respect for Local Traditions

The narrative delves into Walmart's approach to respecting and preserving local traditions. From marketing campaigns to product offerings, the chapter illustrates how Walmart incorporates cultural sensitivity into its global business practices.

Global Workforce Dynamics

As a multinational corporation, Walmart manages a diverse and extensive global workforce. This section explores how the company addresses the unique dynamics of its global employee base.

Cultural Inclusivity in the Workplace

The chapter examines how Walmart fosters cultural inclusivity within its global workforce. Interviews with employees from different regions provide insights into the challenges and successes of building a diverse and harmonious workplace.

Cross-Cultural Leadership Development

The narrative explores Walmart's strategies for developing cross-cultural leadership. Case studies illustrate instances where Walmart invests in leadership programs to cultivate a cadre of leaders capable of navigating the complexities of a global business environment.

Technology Transfer and Innovation Exchange

This section explores how Walmart contributes to technology transfer and innovation exchange on a global scale.

International Technology Partnerships

The chapter examines Walmart's international technology partnerships. From collaborations with tech companies to joint ventures with local innovators, the narrative illustrates how Walmart fosters technology transfer and innovation in diverse global markets.

Global Innovation Hubs

The narrative delves into Walmart's establishment of global innovation hubs. Case studies highlight instances where Walmart collaborates with local talent and resources to drive innovation and technological advancements in various regions.

The Future of Global Citizenship

As the chapter concludes, it reflects on the evolving landscape of global citizenship and Walmart's role in shaping a responsible and ethical future on a global scale. The narrative offers a synthesis of the global initiatives, challenges, and opportunities explored throughout the book, providing readers with insights into the complexities of navigating a complex and interconnected world.

14

Summary

In this comprehensive exploration of Walmart's impact on the retail landscape, society, and global affairs, the book unfolds across twelve chapters, each delving into a distinct facet of the retail giant's journey. From the foundational narrative of Jim Walton and the rise of the Walmart Empire to the ongoing challenges and innovations of the 21st century, the book navigates through the intricate layers of Walmart's legacy.

The chapters progressively unfold, providing insights into the leadership transitions, global expansions, and technological advancements that have shaped Walmart's trajectory. The narrative delves into the company's commitment to sustainability, corporate responsibility, and the enduring impact it has on local communities. Each chapter paints a vivid picture of Walmart's role as a global influencer, exploring its relationships with suppliers, the complexities of its global operations, and the challenges it faces in the ever-evolving retail landscape.

As the book progresses, it examines Walmart's initiatives in e-commerce, artificial intelligence, and automation, showcasing the company's commitment to staying at the forefront of technological innovation. The narrative also reflects on the social, economic, and cultural impact of Walmart on local communities, shedding light on the intricate dynamics of its relationships with small businesses, its role in job creation, and its cultural significance.

Chapters dedicated to Walmart's global influence provide an in-depth look at the company's role in international diplomacy, trade relations, and philanthropy. The book addresses Walmart's contributions to global humanitarian efforts, its initiatives in climate action, and its commitment to ethical sourcing and human rights.

The later chapters delve into Walmart's strategies for community-centric development, exploring how the company empowers local communities through technological initiatives, health and wellness programs, and educational empowerment. The book also explores Walmart's role as a global citizen, addressing the challenges of cultural sensitivity, ethical supply chains, and the dynamics of its diverse global workforce.

The concluding chapters offer a forward-looking perspective, examining Walmart's vision for the future, its strategies for sustainable development, and its evolving role in global citizenship. The narrative reflects on the challenges and opportunities that lie ahead, providing readers with a comprehensive understanding of Walmart's ongoing narrative as a global retail leader and its multifaceted impact on society, economies, and the world.